THE DYING CAVE

A Park Pals Mystery

Book 3

Dwain Cassady

LAP CAT
PUBLISHING

THE
DYING
CAVE

CHAPTER 1

She was tired of pacing the eight foot by eight foot room. She was tired of banging her fists against the walls. She was all cried out. Lying face-down on the bed, she wished she were anywhere but here.

Her hands were sore, bruised from repeated sessions of hammering the walls in hopes of getting help. Her throat was sore and hoarse from screaming.

No windows. No door. Just four walls, three cots, a chair, and a TV. At least there's a TV.

She had tried not to turn on the TV at first. *I don't want to give them the idea I'm enjoying myself.* Finally, boredom had forced her to rethink that strategy.

I wonder if it's day or night. This is going to drive me insane. At least they feed me and let me out long enough to go to the bathroom. I think I saw daylight the last time I was out.

Her body stiffened when she heard the telltale sounds.

They're coming. Again.

CHAPTER 2

The campfire was miserably warm. The muggy August evening in Gainesville, GA, had Fitz and Zee sitting farther back than usual.

"Maybe a campfire wasn't the best idea," Fitz said, not liking the heat. He tugged his salt and pepper beard, then slid his chair farther from the fire.

"But it sho' is purdy, and I think the smoke is helpin' keep the bugs away," Zee replied as he moved his chair to get out of the smoke again. He sat his long, lanky self down next to Fitz, pulled off his hat, and ran a hand through the tight curls of his newly cropped hair.

Fitz and Zee, both residentially challenged and living out of their vehicles, had decided to meet at Fitz's favorite spot, a cul-de-sac on the lake, and spend the evening together. This was part of Luna's quest to help Fitz overcome loneliness and isolation. She had suggested the idea, and Fitz couldn't decline with Zee right there. So here they sat.

Fitz's ginger cat, Buffett, sniffed around the area. He was on his leash. Zee's dog, King, wandered about freely.

The smoke changed direction and headed toward Zee. When he moved, the smoke aimed at Fitz, and he joined Zee on the other side of the fire, pulling Buffett along.

"Ya reckon the smoke does that on purpose? It seems like it knows where we are," Zee observed.

"I don't think it's that smart. It probably has something to do with wind and airflow."

"I wish I'd thought to bring stuff to make s'mores."

"That would be good. I can't remember the last time I had one of those ... probably back in my twenties," Fitz chuckled.

They sat in silence, watching the fire. Zee sipped on the wine in his thermos, and Fitz sipped on a soda.

"You ever married?" Zee asked.

"I don't want to talk about it."

"That's supposed to be why we're here ... to talk."

Buffett jumped up into Fitz's lap and purred. Fitz stared into the fire. The crackling wood and dancing flames worked some kind of magic, softening his heart. He opened the little drawstring pouch he kept around his neck. It kept his stash of dark chocolate M&Ms from melting as they would in his pocket during the summer. He pulled out a few M&Ms and popped them into his mouth.

"OK. I've never been married. I was in love, but she died in Kuwait. An IED. I still have her picture in my wallet."

Fitz looked up, and the waxing gibbous moon looked back. "She said that whenever I see the moon, I can remember that she is with me."

"I'm sorry, Fitz. That's a sad tale."

"How about you? Were you ever married?" Fitz asked, wanting to get his mind and the conversation off Sharon … if he could.

Zee grinned. "You know a good looking guy like me had to get married."

"What happened.?" Fitz asked.

"I guess it's a night for sad stories. You got a tissue?"

Fitz laughed. "I don't think I'll need one."

"OK. Here goes. I was married to a wonderful woman. We had a wonderful daughter. When she was thirty-one, she came down with an aggressive form of breast cancer. At thirty-two it took her.

"That's when I started drinkin'. You can probably guess the rest of the story from here. My wife and I couldn't hold it together, so we split up. I was so depressed, I didn't even try to find a place to live, just stayed in my car. And I'm still here today."

He stretched his arms. "Seems like a long time ago. I guess it was. It's hard to keep up, but I think it's been six years now. Need a tissue yet?"

Fitz looked over to Zee, then reached out and patted his shoulder. "I'm sorry you lost your daughter. That had to have been brutal."

"It's the worst thing I've ever been through. Nobody should have to lose a daughter. Look at us, two old sad sorts sittin' here by a beautiful fire. Surely we can find somethin' happy to talk about," Zee said. "At least we haven't had any kidnappin's or anybody gettin' shot at lately."

Fitz laughed for the second time that night. "True. I still remember Crystal's face when they marched her into the jail that morning. Seeing her so mad was worth the trouble," he said, remembering when they had caught Crystal Samson forcing the employees of her cleaning company to steal drugs from their clients last spring.

Zee laughed. "That was one ornery woman, but she did have a nice car. I wonder whatever happened to her Vette."

"She's probably trying to find you so she can give it to you," Fitz teased.

"Now, don't go pulling my heartstrings. That's just mean!" Zee chuckled.

"I read the other day that her trial is scheduled to start the end of next month," Fitz added.

"It's sad to think she's still roaming free, driving that white Corvette. I wish they'd hurry up and put that one away. She's a bad apple."

"I think you're the one who pointed out that the wheels of justice grind slowly."

"Sounds like some of my wisdom," Zee chuckled. King nudged his hand. "You want another biscuit?"

Zee dug into his pocket and handed over the treat. As soon as King took it, Buffett hopped into his lap. "You, too, huh?" Zee reached into the other pocket and fished out a few cat treats. "It'd be easier if y'all ate the same treats."

The fire began to burn down and the heat of the day eased a bit. Frogs provided loud background music, and the moon reflected off the lake.

"It's nice sittin' here," Zee said. "Makes me feel close to nature."

"Yeah, it is." Fitz agreed. "Beating the heat is a tough job in the summer. Have you found any tricks that help?"

"I'm sure you know where the shady spots are around town," Zee answered.

"Yeah, I keep an eye out for those. I'd spend more time in the library if it weren't for Buffett. He'd get too hot in the car, though."

Zee chuckled. "We do have to keep the critters cool. Hey, maybe they'd let us bring 'em into the library as emotional support pets."

"You try first, and we'll see what happens," Fitz replied.

With the fire totally out, Fitz looked at his watch. It was 10:44. "It's past time for Buffett and me to turn in. How about you?"

"I'll settle down right after I finish my wine. Cain't afford to waste it."

With a chuckle and a stretch, Fitz asked, "Do you want me to wake you up in the morning before I head to the park?"

"Nah. I have a built-in alarm. King never lets me sleep late."

"Same with Buffett. I'll see you at the park then."

CHAPTER 3

The mean sun started early, heating the world as soon as it broke the horizon. At Laurel Park, Fitz had already washed up at the restroom and was through tending to Buffett's needs when Zee rolled in.

"Whooowee! It's gonna be a hot one today," Zee said as he unfolded his lanky frame and stood from the car, a process that took time because of his sore joints.

"I believe you're right," Fitz replied. "Did you sleep good?"

"Like a baby. Neither me nor King has a guilty conscience that keeps us awake. How about you?"

"Fair. Talking about Sharon got me to thinking about her and missing her again."

"Sorry, man. She must have meant a lot to you."

"Yeah. Still does."

"You know, I need to get me an SUV like yours. My car's too low to the ground, and I might not be able to get out of it much longer. Want to trade?"

Fitz chuckled. "No, thanks. I have this one all organized."

Fitz pulled out the insulated travel mug that he kept stuffed with ice and M&Ms and loaded a handful of M&Ms into the little drawstring pouch.

"You're as crazy about those M&Ms as I am about wine," Zee laughed.

While Zee was in the bathroom cleaning up, three headlights bobbed in the dim morning light as the cars went over the speed hump and headed toward Fitz. Ben Blessing, Luna Castillo, and Katía Bancroft pulled in right behind each other.

Zee walked out just as they parked. "Perfect timin'."

"Good morning, guys!" Luna said as she bounced out of her 4Runner, her raven-colored hair in a ponytail that she had pulled through the opening in the back of her baseball cap. "Did you have a good time last night?"

"It was marvelous," Zee replied. "We enjoyed sittin' 'round the campfire and chattin' about our sob stories … at least I did."

Luna looked to Fitz, eyebrows raised.

"It was nice," he said. "But it did stir up some old memories."

"Well, I'm glad you two had fun," she replied.

Ben, gray-haired with a neatly trimmed beard, unloaded Snickers, a light brown labradoodle, from the back of his Outback. Snickers made a beeline to Zee, sniffing for treats.

"Of course I have your biscuit," Zee said, delivering the delicious morsel. "OK, you can have another one," he said to King, his small brown mutt.

Buffett meowed from the back of Fitz's old Highlander.

"I didn't forget you, either," Zee said and placed some cat treats on the floor of the vehicle. Buffett purred while gobbling them down.

"You're a popular guy among the critters," Katía noted as she pulled her unruly black hair into a pony tail.

"It's my animal magnetism," Zee chuckled.

"Let's start walking before it gets any hotter. I don't want to glisten too much," Luna said.

Fitz finished snapping Buffett's harness, and the five humans and three critters headed for the trail.

"Summer's my favorite season, but not when it's this hot," Katía said. "It's supposed to hit ninety-eight today."

"I hate summers," Fitz grumbled.

"How come?" Ben asked.

"I can do things to stay warm in the winter, but there's no way to escape the heat," Fitz answered.

"Yeah, that has to be hard. How do you manage?" Ben replied.

"If I didn't have Buffett, I'd spend a lot of time at the library, but I can't just leave him in the car. Mostly we hunt the shady spots around town."

"Yeah, we know 'em by heart," Zee added. "I'll probably go take a dip in the lake at Clarks Bridge sometime this afternoon."

"Today is going to be the hottest so far," Ben said. "Why don't you come spend the afternoon with me? The host isn't much, but the AC works."

"That's kind of you, Ben. I might take you up on it," Fitz said.

"Me and King'll be there," Zee said, rubbing his hands together.

The crew rounded a curve in the trail that was right at the lake, and Snickers started whining and pulling toward the water.

"Oh, no, you don't," Ben said. "I don't want you all wet and nasty."

He tried to continue walking, but Snickers kept straining toward the lake, then she started barking.

"Look at that. Someone threw a water bottle into the lake. I don't know why people have to litter," Katía said.

"I think Snickers wants to get it and clean up the lake," Zee noted.

Ben rubbed his free hand through his beard and huffed. "OK, girl. If it's that important to you." He unleashed Snickers, and she bounded into the water, swimming straight toward the bottle.

"It looks like you're right, Zee," Luna said.

They watched as Snickers grabbed the bottle and swam back to shore. After a good shake, she trotted up to Ben and handed over the bottle.

"Well, aren't you the environmentally conscious one," Ben said. "I guess we'll have to recycle this since you went to all that trouble."

"There's a piece of paper inside," Katía noted.

"Ooh! What if it's a message from a long lost lover?" Luna said.

"Highly unlikely," Fitz replied.

"I am curious to see if it's a note, though," Katía added.

"OK," Ben said, handing the wet bottle to Katía.

She unscrewed the top and shook the bottle upside down. The paper had expanded and wouldn't come out. "It's stuck," she said.

"Hold on a minute," Ben said, fishing in his pocket. He pulled out a small Swiss Army knife that had a pair of tweezers. With the bottle upside down, he was able to catch the corner of the paper and pull it just out of the bottle. "Can you get it before I let go?" he asked Katía.

She caught hold. As she started to pull, Luna said, "Don't tear it."

With a few twists, Katía was able to work the paper out of the bottle. The others, except for Fitz, crowded in as she unrolled it. Written in hurried letters was the message:

HELP!

*I'M 16, AND I'M TRAPPED
IN A HOUSE NEAR THE LAKE.
IT'S A FARM.*

SADIE

With wide eyes, Luna said, "Fitz, look at this. A girl needs help."

Katía handed over the message. Fitz's eyebrows scrunched as he read. "Probably just a prank," he said, though he had an uneasy feeling in his gut.

"How can you say that? It looks like it was written in distress," Luna said. "Being a teacher, I know a thing or two about handwriting."

"It just ain't right for anyone to lose a daughter," Zee said, mouth drawn. He rubbed his hands over the top of his head. "We gotta do somethin'."

"What could we possibly do?" Fitz asked, his free fist tightening.

"Call the police, for one," Luna said, pulling her phone from her back pocket.

"I wonder how old this is," Fitz said, his fist still clenched as he handed the note back to Katía.

"Looks pretty new to me," Zee observed.

Luna had already dialed 911. "I need to report a teen who has been abducted." She went on to explain how they had found the note, then gave their location.

Disconnecting, she said, "They're sending a deputy out."

Fitz dug some M&Ms out of the little pouch and ate them.

"I guess we're waiting for the deputy instead of walking today," Ben said.

CHAPTER 4

The park pals watched as the patrol car came down the road. As it pulled into a parking place, Zee elbowed Ben in the ribs. "That's the deputy that arrested us last spring!"

Diann James exited the patrol car and walked toward the waiting group. Her serious face broke into a grin when she saw Zee. "I believe I had the pleasure of arresting you once before. ... and if it isn't the infamous Fitz Fitzgerald. I'm Diann James. I assume you folks made the call since you're the only ones here."

"Yes, I made the call," Luna said. She stepped forward and shook the deputy's hand. "We found, well technically Snickers found this bottle in the lake. It had a note inside. We think a young lady is in trouble." Katía handed over the note.

Deputy James's eyes narrowed as she read, then she seemed to relax. "They even went to the trouble to make it look like they were writing in a hurry with a shaky hand. Look, this was most likely a group of kids out joyriding in their boat, then decided throwing this out would be a cute prank." She handed the note back.

"Deputy, I don't mean to be disrespectful," Zee said, "But somebody's daughter really could be in trouble. Cain't you at least check it out?"

Fitz spoke up. "It wouldn't hurt to check the missing persons database to see if anyone by that name is on the list."

"OK," Deputy James said, pulling out a notepad. "What was the name?"

"Sadie," Katía replied. She handed the deputy her business card. "Please let me know what you find out."

She handed the card back. "Thanks, but I won't need that. I'm going to check on it right now. Hang on a couple of minutes." She returned to her car to work on the computer.

Zee rubbed the top of his head. "I hope she's right about it bein' a prank."

"What if she finds a Sadie on the report? What are we going to do?" Ben asked.

"Hunt down the sorry soul that kidnapped her," Fitz replied.

After a few minutes, Deputy James got out of the car, bringing the computer with her. "This doesn't mean anything, but there is a Sadie Langston listed. She disappeared from Palestine, Texas, three weeks ago." She held up the computer with a picture of the girl, who had wavy brunette hair and green eyes.

Zee rubbed the top of his head. "Oh, no."

"Like I said, this is probably just a coincidence. There are a lot of girls named Sadie around here, too. I am going to need the bottle and note as evidence, though."

She closed the computer and held out a plastic bag. Ben deposited the bottle. Katía took a photo, then added the note.

"Thank you. We'll be checking for any suspicious activity." Deputy James said.

Katía held out her business card again. "Please keep me updated."

Deputy James accepted the card this time. "I'll do what I can, but we don't typically comment on ongoing investigations."

"Well, now what?" Ben asked as Deputy James drove away.

"We have to find that girl," Zee said.

"I was afraid someone was going to say that," Ben replied.

"You realize she could be anywhere between here and the headwaters of the Chattahoochee," Fitz said.

"No, the note says she's in a house near the lake. That narrows it down," Ben observed.

"The house was obviously close enough for her to get the bottle into the water, so it must be a lake house," Luna added.

"And just how many houses are there between here and the north end of the lake?" Fitz asked, stuffing his hands into his pockets as anger rose at his frustration over the possibility that someone had abducted this girl. "There is no way we're going to find her, if she even exists."

"Well, I'm gonna try, even if I have to knock on every door of every house on the lake. I know what it's like to lose a daughter, and I don't want anyone else to have to go through that," Zee said. He started walking toward his car.

"Where are you going?" Fitz asked.

"I'm gonna start on the west side and work my way north."

"Good grief," Fitz said. "Come back. We need to come up with a plan. If you knock on the door and ask if they have an abducted teen, what do you think they'll say?"

"I'd lie like a dog," Zee said, returning to the group. "No offense, King. So what else can we do?"

"Let's go to the pavilion and get out of the sun," Luna suggested.

Fitz worked his mind as he walked, Buffett prancing just ahead of him. *This is ridiculous. We'll never find her. I can't even imagine how to start. I have to come up with an idea. I wish the note had given us more to go on. I really hate child predators.* The event that got him fired for using excessive force in an arrest flashed into his mind. That man had been a child predator, too. He realized Katía was talking.

"Why would someone go all the way to Texas to abduct a girl?" Katía asked.

"The farther away they take her, the less likely she is to be found, maybe," Ben answered.

"True. No one is likely to recognize her here," Luna added.

"Zee's idea might be the best," Ben said. "If we split up and knock on doors, we can at least get a feel for anyone who seems suspicious."

"Do you think the Sheriff's Department will actually do anything?" Luna asked.

"I'm sure they'll search a few reports to see if they find any leads. I doubt they'll go out searching house to house because they just don't have the manpower for that," Fitz said.

"In that case, it's up to us." Zee started walking toward his car again.

"Wait, Zee," Fitz called. "Trying to canvass every house on the lake isn't the answer. We have to narrow it down."

"There are a lot of houses, but there can't be that many farms on the lake," Katía noted.

"Yeah. Let me pull up the map and see if we can identify tracts of land that look like farms," Ben suggested.

"You start at the north end, and I'll start here at the park," Luna added.

"I'll look, too," Katía said.

Zee put his hand up to block the sun and scanned across the lake. "She could be right over there… somewhere."

"Wow! There is a lot of empty land north of Don Carter State Park. Most of it's covered in trees. … Wait, here is an area that's cleared. It could be pastureland," Ben said. "There's another one. And another."

"I see two potential sites," Luna added.

Fitz was tapping on his phone as they were identifying potential farms.

"What do you think, Fitz?" Ben asked. "It looks like we have five potential sites."

"We have a photo, too," Fitz said, having located Sadie's picture on the web. He held up the phone.

"Great! Text that to us," Katía said.

Fitz looked at the phone and ran his fingers through his beard.

"Hand over the phone," Katía chuckled. "I'll show you how to do it." She pulled up the group text, showed Fitz how to add the photo, and hit send. "Voila!"

"We could get through this a lot quicker if we split up," Ben suggested.

"Why don't Ben, Zee, and I hit the two on the east side of the lake while Fitz and Katía hit the three on the west side?" Luna said.

"Sounds like a plan to me," Katía answered.

Fitz tugged on his beard. "This is a long shot, but let's get going."

"I'll be happy to drive. You can bring Buffett so he won't get too hot," Katía said.

The group split up to take their chances on finding the girl.

CHAPTER 5

Fitz studied the map while Katía drove slowly along Glade Forest Road, where Ben had identified two potential farms. It was a peaceful, winding country road.

"Wait! That was it," Fitz announced right after they had passed the mailbox.

Katía turned around and pulled into the gravel drive. It led to an older one-story brick home that was well kept. When she parked, she said, "I say we tell them that the daughter of a friend of ours is missing and ask if they have seen her. Their reaction could tell us a lot."

"That's exactly what I was thinking," Fitz replied.

"Great minds, you know," Katía chuckled.

Fitz knocked on the door and stepped back. He automatically reached to pull out his former badge. *I wonder if I'll ever stop doing that.*

The door opened to reveal an elderly man with a cane. "Hello," he said.

"Hi, sir. The daughter of a friend of ours has gone missing. We're trying to help find her and were wondering if you had seen this girl." Katía held up her phone with the photo open. "Her name is Sadie Langston."

"No, I don't believe I've seen her. My wife and I don't get out much, though, so we don't run into many people."

"Thank you very much. I hope you have a good day," Katía replied, then headed back to her Prius.

"Stay put, Buffett," Fitz ordered as he got into the car.

"I think we can check them off the list of suspects," Katía said as she turned the car around to leave.

"Yeah, they don't give me the criminal vibe," Fitz replied.

"Is there such a thing?"

"Yeah. You can just sense it in people. The next one looks to be about half a mile up the road. I'll try to warn you before we pass it this time." He pulled out a small notebook and started writing.

"What are you doing?" Katía asked.

"Jotting down some notes."

"There are only three houses. I don't think you need notes to keep track of that."

"You'd be surprised what I can forget … or what trivial detail might be important later." He resumed writing.

Fitz pointed to the driveway as they approached. "That's it."

Katía turned in and stopped. "This gives me the creeps."

The driveway curved around trees, and they couldn't see the house at first. On the right side, a fence surrounded a pasture where a few cows munched on grass. The driveway was two ruts, badly in need of gravel, with tall grass in the center.

"Do you think this place is abandoned?" Katía asked.

"There's not but one way to find out. Keep going," Fitz replied.

"OK." Katía crept around the curve to find an old white clapboard farm house with a wraparound porch on the left side. Beyond the house was a red barn. An older red Chevy pickup with a crew cab sat near the barn.

"It could use a coat of paint," Fitz said, approaching the house.

Before they got to the steps leading to the front porch, the door opened.

"Can I help you?" a tall, lanky young man with blue eyes, jet black hair, and a bushy beard asked.

"I certainly hope so," Katía said. "The daughter of a friend of ours is missing, and we're trying to help find her." Katía kept marching up the steps. Fitz stood back to observe.

Fitz noticed the man's back stiffen and his head pull slightly back.

"I don't know about any missing girls." He started closing the door.

"Could you look at her picture to be sure?" Katía continued approaching.

She held up her phone, and the young man put his head through the opening of the door.

"Nah. Ain't seen her. Now I'll kindly ask you'uns to get off my property."

"Is there anybody else here we could show the photo to?" Katía asked to the closing door.

"Let's do as he asked and go," Fitz said.

Katía lingered on the porch, hand poised to knock again.

"Come on," Fitz urged, his voice a low growl.

She turned, let the screen door slam, and stomped down the steps. "That was one grumpy soul," she said as she followed Fitz.

Fitz didn't say a word. *I wish she'd hold her tongue till we get in the car.*

Once the car doors were closed, Katía fumed, "He definitely goes on the suspect list."

"Maybe," Fitz replied. "I know a lot of people who'd react that way to strangers on their property."

"That's true but still, I'm suspicious. I definitely got that criminal vibe. Where's the next one?" she huffed as she drove out the driveway.

"It's on Belton Bridge Road. Take a left when you come to the stop sign."

Buffett hopped into Fitz's lap. "What do you think, Buffett? Could that guy have been a kidnapper?"

"Meow."

"I see. Buffett says add him to the list."

Katía chuckled. "I'm glad we agree, Buffett." She gave his head a quick rub. "Let's see if we find another crazy at the next place."

* * * * *

Ben pulled up to the first house they were checking. "Wow! I wonder how much this place is worth."

"In the millions, I'm sure," Luna replied.

"Whee doggies! I could live in a place like this," Zee added, rubbing his hands together.

"Looks like they make their own wine," Ben noted, observing the heavy grapes just beginning to ripen.

"I think I've found heaven," Zee said.

"Don't drool on the porch while we're waiting," Ben chuckled. He parked in the drive that circled around the front of the house. Another drive branched off and led to a three-car garage. Beyond the grape vines running along the side of the house, the lake reflected the morning sun.

"This doesn't look like the home of a child predator," Luna said.

"You never know," Ben said. "That could be how they got enough money to build this place."

"That's creepy but true," Luna replied as they got out to go to the door.

Walking up the steps, Ben said, "Smile pretty. We're being recorded." He stepped up to the door and pushed the Ring doorbell. A low "Woof," sounded from inside.

"That sounds like a big dog," Zee observed. "I'm glad King's in the car."

"Hello. How may I help you?" came through the speaker. It was a man's voice with a hint of irritation.

"We're looking for a missing teenage girl and are canvassing the neighborhood to see if anyone might have spotted her," Ben replied.

"Do you have a photo?" the voice asked.

"I do."

"If you'll point it toward the camera, I'll have a look."

Luna stepped forward and aimed her phone at the Ring.

"No, I can't say that I have seen the young lady. Sorry. If you will, please leave … now."

Ben replied, "Thanks for your help." He turned and walked back to the car, not surprised that they struck out.

As they were pulling out of the driveway, Luna said, "He seemed a bit grumpy. Do you think he's hiding something?"

"He was probably working and not happy about the interruption," Ben answered.

"Man, I should've asked if I could stay with them," Zee moaned. "I'd be willin' to work a bit if ole Arthur'd let me."

"Want me to turn around? I'm sure they'll take you in."

"Nah. That big dog would probably eat me anyway."

"Why would someone with that much money need to work?" Luna wondered.

Their next stop turned out to be a horse farm, complete with a plantation-style two-story white house. A chestnut horse trotted over to the fence as they got out, eyeing them with a hopeful look.

"Look at that cutie pie," Luna said. She got out and went straight to the horse. "Sorry, I don't have any goodies for you," she said as she patted its neck.

"That sure looks invitin'," Zee said, eyeing the hammock swing on the front porch. "Y'all come back in a couple of hours after I've had a nap."

"Zee, we're on a mission, remember?" Luna scolded.

Ben led the way again and knocked on the door.

"I hope they invite us in. I'd love to see the inside of this place," Luna said while they waited.

After about a minute, Ben knocked again. "There might not be anyone home."

"Hola," a stocky, fit man called as he strode toward the porch, a couple of pieces of straw stuck to his jeans. He appeared to be in his early sixties. Taking off a straw hat, he rubbed his forehead with his sleeve.

Thinking it odd that the man had on long sleeves in this heat, Ben went through his spiel about looking for the abducted girl. Luna showed him the photo.

"Bonita ... but no, I have not seen her," the man replied.

Assuming he was a stable hand, Ben asked, "Have you heard any cries for help coming from the house?"

"Just me when my wife's mad at me," he replied with a laugh. "I'm Emilio Sánchez. Welcome to my little patch of paradise."

"You have a beautiful place here," Luna said.

"Do you mind if I have a nap in your hammock?" Zee asked.

Emilio laughed while Luna huffed, "Zee!"

"You nap as long as you want, my friend," Emilio replied.

"Thanks for your help, and we'll take Zee off your hands," Ben said.

* * * * *

Fitz pointed to the driveway of their next target, and Katía turned into it. Elaborate rock pillars supported a closed gate.

"Do you think I should push the intercom button?" Katía asked.

"Yeah. There's no other way to find out if they know anything about this girl."

Katía had to undo her seatbelt and lean out the window to reach the button.

Fitz scanned the property while they waited. "What does that remind you of?" He pointed.

"Crystal Samson's wedding venue," Katía replied, noting the row of four outbuildings. "Brings back not so fond memories of our last adventure."

The intercom came to life with a woman's voice. "How might I help you?"

"We're trying to locate a missing girl and would like to ask if you have seen her," Katía answered.

"I haven't."

Irritated, Katía replied, "How do you know if you don't look at her picture?"

"Look, I'm trying to work. I don't know anything about a missing girl."

The intercom went dead, and the gate stayed shut.

CHAPTER 6

Still parked at the elaborate gate, Katia pulled out her phone and began typing something in.

"What are you doing?" Fitz asked. "They want us to get out of here."

"I'm giving her a chance to change her mind."

"Oh."

"I'm also texting Luna to let her know we're on our way back to the park."

"Oh," Fitz said pulling on his beard. After pulling three M&Ms from his pouch, he added, "I don't want to get arrested for loitering or stalking or whatever they would claim we're doing."

"OK. I'm done, and the gate didn't open." Katía drove toward the park. "Do you think we struck out?"

"Not totally. We know of at least two grumpy characters. It's possible they could be hiding something. It's also possible they're just goats."

"If we were the police, what would be the next step?" Katía asked.

Fitz tugged his beard again and thought back to his police days. "I'd send a boat by to look for suspicious activity from the water side."

Katía tightened her grip on the wheel and sat up straighter. "That's brilliant! We need a boat!"

"Oh."

They arrived at Laurel Park to find Ben, Luna, and Zee under a pavilion poring over a map of the lake.

"Zee had a great idea," Luna said as Fitz and Katía walked up, being led by Buffett. "We should take Carlos's boat and check out these houses from the water. We didn't get very far by knocking on the doors."

"That's exactly what Fitz said," Katía replied.

Fitz tugged his beard. He wasn't particularly fond of water, and the boat would be on water.

"Zee did find paradise, though." Ben added.

"And what did paradise look like?" Katía asked.

"One of the places makes their own wine. I could be a live-in wine taster!"

"Did you turn up anything?" Ben asked.

"Just one nice older couple and a couple of grumps," Fitz replied. "I think we can strike the older couple off the list of suspects. The other two, maybe, but they really just seemed not to want to be bothered by strangers."

"I'm more suspicious than Fitz," Katía said. "The last one wouldn't even open the gate so we could show them the picture. I think they're prime suspects, but the other guy gave me the creeps. I'm keeping him on the list, too."

"One of our folks turned out to be a nice guy with a horse farm," Luna said. "The other just talked to us through the intercom. He seemed irritated that we were there. I'd consider him a possibility."

"Three out of five potential suspects," Ben observed. "At least we've narrowed it down by forty percent."

Luna's phone pinged. "Carlos said he'll be happy to take us out tomorrow. He said let's leave at ten, so he'll have time to get the boat cleaned up and gassed."

The next morning, Fitz and Zee drove to Ben's house after their morning walk. Neither King nor Buffett would be happy on the boat, so they were going to stay at the house to keep from overheating.

"Thanks for letting us leave the critters here," Fitz said.

"Yeah, that's mighty kind of you," Zee agreed.

"You're more than welcome. Snickers will enjoy the company. She'd love the boat ride, but I don't want to risk her barking if we happen to find this girl," Ben said.

Ben drove them to the boat ramp, where they found Carlos, Luna, and Katía already launching the boat. Fitz got out of the car and froze. He hadn't thought about the women wearing swimsuits, but there they were. He was glad they were wearing wraps. Ben and Carlos wore swim trunks and t-shirts.

Fitz looked at Zee, and Zee shrugged. "I didn't know we was goin' swimmin'."

"Me, either," Fitz replied. He was wearing his jeans and a t-shirt that said, "GA TECH."

Katía waved, "Good morning! It's a glorious day!"

"Good mornin'," Zee called back. He, Ben, and Fitz joined Katía on the dock as Carlos was pulling up the boat. Katía ran to hug the others as she usually did.

Fitz stiffened, then lightly patted her on the back. "It's good to see you, too."

"I brought us a picnic lunch," Luna said, returning from the parking lot. "We can eat out on the lake! I love a lake picnic!"

She stopped and put her hands on her hips. "Where are your swimsuits? You'll burn up out there in blue jeans."

"Sorry, but I don't own a swimsuit," Fitz replied.

"Oh. Sorry, I shouldn't have said that." Luna patted him on the shoulder. "Let's hop aboard."

Carlos puttered through the no wake zone, then took off. Fitz tightened the chinstrap on his hat against the wind. Carlos had to slow down for another no wake zone as they came to Clarks Bridge. Swallow nests lined the side of the bridge.

The two houses that Ben, Luna, and Zee had visited came up first.

"I think that's it," Luna said, pointing ahead.

Katía pulled binoculars from the bag she had brought. "Nice place. I see the grape vines Zee was so excited about. Looks like they'll be getting ripe in a few weeks.

"Put down the binoculars. Here comes a boat," Ben said.

Katía lowered them but kept scanning the property. "I don't see anything suspicious. When that boat gets by, I'll try to see through the windows."

"That's a creepy thing to do," Luna said.

"We'll never know if Sadie is in there if I don't," Katía replied.

"True. Spy away," Luna answered.

Fitz sat back, glad he had brought sunglasses, and enjoyed the rocking of the boat as the wake passed through. Looking over the manicured grounds and neatly kept vineyard, he had a hunch. "I don't believe we're going to find anything here."

Katía held on to the windshield of the runabout. "I won't be able to focus until the boat stops rocking." As soon as the wake passed, she resumed her mission.

"I see a man sitting at the kitchen table. It looks like he's drinking coffee. Oh, no. It looks like he's looking at me looking at him."

"I think it's time to go," Fitz said.

Carlos throttled up the engine, and they headed to the next house.

When he stopped the boat, Fitz pulled out his notebook and wrote: *House 1. Vineyard. Seems unlikely to be involved.* Looking up, he saw a two-story dock with a large pontoon boat on lifts. Beyond the dock, there was a barn and three horses grazing in a pasture in the distance. Katía was already searching with the binoculars.

"This is the place with the nice man. I don't think he's a kidnapper," Ben said.

"Their curtains are all drawn. I can't see anything inside," Katía groaned.

"That's probably to prevent people on the lake from gawking at them," Ben chuckled. He consulted the map. "The next house is a good ways up. It's past Don Carter State Park."

Carlos aimed the boat north and piloted it through the progressively narrowing, winding lake.

"Slow down," Luna called. "I've never seen the park from the water."

Carlos slowed the boat as they passed by the dock and small beach the park afforded. He sped up once they had passed the park, and Fitz and Katía searched the shoreline for the first house they had visited.

"Wait! I think we just passed it," Katía called over the engine noise.

Carlos turned around, and Katía pointed. The house peeked through trees about a hundred yards from the shore.

"Isn't that it, Fitz?" Katía asked.

"It looks right," he answered. "This is the older couple that we didn't think would be involved," he added.

While Katía searched with the binoculars, Fitz wrote in his notebook: *House 2. Horse farm. Nice guy. House 3. Older couple. Not likely.*

"I can sort of see into the kitchen, but it's dark. I don't see anyone. The next house is where we met the grumpy young guy. I think it has more potential," Katía said.

"Let's check out the last two houses, then we can find a spot for lunch and a swim," Luna suggested.

CHAPTER 7

A passing cloud took pity on Fitz and blocked the searing sun. He felt instant relief and wiped sweat from his forehead.

Carlos pointed ahead. "What's that in the water?"

"It's a cow!" Luna exclaimed as the boat got closer. "There's another one coming down the bank."

"I cain't say as I've ever seen that before," Zee said.

"I think they're from the next house we want to see," Katía said.

The cow eyed them as Carlos stopped the boat, then resumed quenching her thirst.

Fitz scanned the property and noted a large vegetable garden that boasted tomatoes, beans, corn, and okra. An old red barn sat to the side between the lake and the house. It was in need of painting like the house.

"Pull up a little farther so I can see all of the house," Katía said.

"There comes a guy with a bucket," Luna said. "It looks like he might be going to pick some vegetables.

"That's not the same guy that answered the door," Katía said. "This one looks younger."

"He's got the same color hair and bushy beard," Fitz observed. "Might be a brother."

"There's another one comin' from the barn," Zee said.

Katía trained the binoculars on him. "I think that's another brother. He's too short to be the one that answered the door. They watched as the guy leaving the barn opened the gate and joined the other one in the garden.

"Gettin' their outside work done before it gets too hot," Zee observed.

"You'd better put down the binoculars before they see you," Fitz said.

"How else am I supposed to find that girl?" Katía hmphed.

"One of them just spotted us," Ben said.

"I know, let's hop in the water like we're cooling down," Luna suggested.

Katía set the binoculars on the seat. "That's a great idea! I am getting hot."

Carlos dived off the bow and splashed into the lake.

Don't stare, Fitz told himself as Katía slipped out of her coverup to reveal a mint one-piece swimsuit. Luna wore a one-piece that was hot pink with a black braided rope pattern. Katía and Luna went to the back of the boat and slipped into the water with noodles.

Fitz and Zee moved to the slight shade afforded by the bimini top. Fitz turned his attention back to the two men in the garden. They worked diligently at the pole beans and appeared not to be paying the boat any attention.

The boat rocked as Carlos climbed the ladder. "Zee, would you toss me the towel under the throttle?"

"Sure," Zee replied.

"That felt good," Luna said as she came aboard. Katía followed right behind. "Do they still seem worried about us?"

"They appear to have forgotten we're out here," Fitz replied. *Don't stare.*

Katía and Luna toweled off, then wrapped themselves in the towels.

"I never have figured out how gals do that," Zee said.

"Do what?" Luna asked.

"Wrap a towel around you and keep it from falling off."

"It's a lady's secret," Luna laughed.

"Zee, could I have that seat a minute?" Katía asked. "I think I can do a little spying without being noticed from there."

Zee moved to the back. "Just when I was gettin' comfortable."

From the shade of the driver's seat, which was on the opposite side of the boat from the house, Katía aimed the binoculars at the windows. Her spine stiffened.

"What is it?" Luna asked.

"There's another man and a girl in there. She looks like she has dark hair like Sadie, but I can't see very well."

"They all have dark hair. It's probably a sister," Fitz said.

"It looks like they're arguing," Katía added.

"I ain't never heard of a brother and sister arguin' before," Zee chuckled.

"I wish I could see her face, but the room's too dark," Katía said.

"The guys are looking. Binoculars down," Fitz urged.

"Let me off at the shore. I'm goin' up there," Zee said. "If it's her, I'm getting' her out of there."

"Hold on, Zee. If it is the girl, they'll probably shoot you before you get near the house," Fitz warned.

Carlos cranked the boat, which had floated close to the shore. "Is it time to head to the next house?"

"Sounds good to me," Ben said. "Let's go before Zee does something rash. Besides, it's hot just sitting here."

"It should be right about here," Ben called, comparing the map to the landmarks.

"I don't see it," Katía replied as she scanned the area for the house where the woman wouldn't let them through the gate.

"Now that I think of it, I don't remember seeing the lake from the driveway," Fitz added.

"This one was eerie. It had outbuildings that reminded us of Crystal's wedding venue," Katía said.

"Does that look like the roofline?" Fitz asked, pointing toward a roof just peeking over the trees.

"Could be," Katía said.

"Not much of a lake view," Ben added.

"Wait, there it is," Katía pointed up ahead to where the trees had been cleared all the way to the lake, leaving an ugly scar.

Carlos pulled the boat slowly forward till they were even with the house.

"Those outbuildings would be the perfect spot to hide someone," Luna said.

"Unless they're air-conditioned, I don't think anyone would survive very long in this heat," Ben said.

"Maybe they have the windows open and a fan," Zee groaned. "At least I hope so for that girl's sake."

With binoculars in hand, Katía reported, "I don't see any lights on. It looks like no one's home."

"Let's sneak up and check out those buildings," Zee said. "If she's here, we cain't leave her sufferin'."

"We could hop onto the dock and run up there right quick," Katía suggested.

"Not a good idea," Fitz replied. "I'm sure a place like this has video surveillance of the whole property, even the dock."

"They might see us, but they ain't gonna catch us," Zee said. "I want to find out if she's here."

Fitz shook his head. "Bad idea."

The dock was a double-decker with two slips. One housed a Mastercraft ski boat and the other two jet skis.

Katía nodded to Carlos. "Pull up to the dock, and we'll have a quick peek." She removed the towel and slipped into her coverup.

As Carlos eased the boat next to the dock, Fitz popped M&Ms into his mouth.

"You stay put, Zee. Let Ben and me go, in case we have to make a quick retreat," Katía suggested.

As soon as Katía's second foot hit the dock, barking erupted up the hill. Two German shepherds charged down the back yard.

"I don't think they're after treats," Zee said.

Katía hurried back into the boat, and Carlos pulled away from the dock.

"That was a short trip," Luna added.

"Now I'm really suspicious," Zee said. "There's got to be a way to get up there."

"Rich folks like to make sure they don't lose anything," Fitz observed. "We'd have to kill or tranquilize the dogs to get up to the house."

"Does anyone know a vet we could get tranquilizers from?" Zee asked.

"We're not going to tranquilize any dogs," Fitz huffed. "We'd end up in jail for that. Let's get out of here." He ate a few more M&Ms.

"Let's see if we can find a shady cove and have our picnic while we figure out our next move," Luna suggested.

Carlos dropped the anchor near the shore in a spot that was shaded by trees leaning out over the water in a quest for sunlight. Across the way, kids jumped from a rock about fifteen feet above the lake.

"I hope everyone likes chicken salad," Luna said. "If not, I brought peanut butter and jelly, too." Carlos pulled out a cooler, and Luna distributed the food.

"What's the matter, Zee?" Fitz asked, noticing Zee wasn't eating his sandwich.

"I'm worried that girl is in one of those outbuildin's, and we cain't get to her."

"Well, it's not going to help if you starve yourself," Luna said.

"True. I couldn't have held out much longer anyway. This smells great."

Finishing a bite of sandwich, Katía said, "I think our two most likely suspects are the last two houses we visited. They both have potential, but the farmers just give me the willies. I'd put my bet on them."

"We're not even sure the abducted girl is in Georgia, and you're already deciding who did it," Fitz said. He was trying to stay logical while his anger grew at the possibility they might have uncovered a case of child molestation… or worse. *What else could it point to?*

"I think the heat's gettin' to you," Zee said. "Too many things are linin' up for it to be a coincidence. Just think how bad you'd feel if we don't do anything and that girl dies. There's got to be a way to get around them dogs."

"You could walk up holding treats in both hands," Ben said with a chuckle.

"I'm afraid you'd lose the treats and your hands," Luna noted. "They were charging like they meant business."

A slow smile grew, and Zee said, "I got it!"

"Oh, no," Fitz groaned.

CHAPTER 8

The baking sun cast its final rays across a pink, darkening sky as the park pals met at the boat ramp off Lula Road. The air was thick with humidity.

"Are you sure you guys want to do this?" Carlos asked before launching the boat.

"I'm positive," Zee said. "I cain't live wondering if that girl is there."

"OK. I guess I can visit you in jail," Carlos chuckled.

"I'm too sly to get caught," Zee grinned.

Fitz shook his head. "I don't know why I let you talk me into this."

Carlos backed the boat off the trailer, and Katía said, "I'll call when we get there. It might be hard for us to find it in the dark."

"We'll get into position and be ready," Fitz replied.

Zee led King to Fitz's car. "Hop in," he said. King jumped into the back seat, where Buffett instantly greeted him. Fitz drove them to the tiny Belton Bridge Park, which was just down the road from the house they were targeting.

"What are you going to do if she's not there?" Fitz asked.

"I don't know. Worry some more, I guess," Zee replied.

They waited in silence for a few minutes. "Something tells me we're not going to find her there," Fitz said.

"Could be, but it's worth eliminatin' the possibility. At least for me."

"I understand," Fitz said. *It must be hard losing a daughter. Maybe as bad as losing Sharon.* A nearly full moon rose in the eastern sky. *You knew I was thinking about you, didn't you? It's gotten easier the last few months. My friends from the park have helped.*

"What you studyin' about so hard?" Zee asked.

"Just remembering Sharon. Every time I see the moon, I think about her."

"Yeah. The moon'll always be around."

Fitz jumped when his phone rang. "Hello."

"Hey. We're just about there," Katía said.

"OK, we're pulling out."

Fitz parked the car on the road near the gated driveway, then called Katía back. "We're here."

"Perfect. I see the dock coming up. It looks like there are a couple of lights on in the house. Are you ready for operation Divide and Conquer?"

Fitz laughed. "As ready as I'll ever be."

Turning to Zee, he said. "They're pulling up to the dock."

Zee pulled on a ski mask and put on a headlamp.

"What in the world?" Fitz said.

"I don't want them to be able to recognize me."

"I wish I had thought of that." Fitz put the phone on speaker.

"OK, we're here," Katía said.

The barking dogs confirmed Katía's words.

"They're charging the dock."

"Make sure you get off in time and don't forget the food," Fitz said. "Zee and I are on our way."

Fitz whispered, "Remember to knock on the door at my signal," then followed Zee as he entered the side of the yard and followed the tree line to the line of outbuildings. Zee stopped at the first one as Fitz continued on.

Fitz looked into Zee's headlamp, shielded his eyes, then nodded. He knocked on the door. "Anyone in there?" The silence was broken by Katía's worried voice. "The dogs heard you. They're coming."

"We have to go, Zee! Head to the car while I check the next two!" Fitz urged as he trotted to the next two buildings, stopping briefly to knock and ask if anyone was there.

"I'm comin'. Save yourself!" Zee replied, limping along as Fitz passed. The approaching barks spurred him a little faster.

Fitz looked back. *He's not going to make it!* He turned back, pulling the Beretta from its holster.

"Don't shoot the dogs, man," Zee said as he moved as fast as his old knee would let him.

"Would you rather they eat you for supper?"

The barking stopped as both dogs appeared from behind the outbuilding. Heads down and hackles up, the two dogs approached, growling.

"Just walk normally, Zee," Fitz coaxed. He got between Zee and the dogs and backed up slowly, gun at the ready. The dogs looked at each other, then advanced slowly.

"Good doggies," Fitz said. "We're leaving. Just give us a minute."

Barking erupted from behind Fitz, and the dogs' ears perked up. King had decided to put in his two cents' worth.

"Don't worry about him. He's just a little dog," Fitz said. A root caught his heel, and he nearly fell backwards. The dogs returned their attention to him. One surged forward, then stopped when Fitz aimed the gun at him.

"So you know what this is, huh? You'd better stay back then."

The dogs kept pace with Fitz but didn't attack. He heard the car door open. *Zee made it. Now if they'll just hold off till I get in.* An idea struck, and Fitz pulled a handful of M&Ms from his pouch and threw them at the dogs. While they stopped to sniff the candies, Fitz kept backing until he bumped into the Highlander. He eased his way around the vehicle, not breaking eye contact with the dogs. Finding the door lever, he jerked it open and jumped in.

The dogs split up, barking madly at each of the front doors.

"I think they want us to leave," Zee said.

"Are you guys OK?" Katía asked. Fitz had forgotten the phone was still connected.

"Yeah. We made it by the skin of our teeth."

"You had me worried."

"I bet you weren't nearly as worried as I was," Fitz replied. "We didn't find the girl."

"That's good. I can't imagine how we'd get her out if you had. Since we're so close, Carlos is going to drive us back to the farmers' house. I want to have another look at the girl I saw there."

Fitz disconnected. "I guess you heard."

"Yeah. Maybe they'll have better luck than we did." Zee rubbed his knee.

On the way back to the boat ramp to wait for the others, Fitz said, "I just realized that you're sober tonight."

"Yeah, I can do it when I have to, but it's not nearly as much fun," Zee laughed.

* * * * *

Carlos drove the boat slowly while Katía and Luna scanned the shore for the house. The moon cast a silvery light on everything.

Luna sidled up to Carlos. "This is romantic," she said, leaning into him. "Katía, you should get a beau and we'll go out on the lake on a night with a full moon."

"That's a tall order. I haven't had a beau in a long time," Katía replied. "And don't go trying to fix me up with someone. It will happen in God's time."

"OK, but if I run across any good prospects, can I at least tell you about them?"

"You and everyone at the church. I believe I'm fix-up proof."

Luna laughed. "Like you said, it will happen in God's time. That just hasn't gotten here yet. Sometimes God needs a little help, though."

"Luna, behave yourself. I think she's trying to tell you to mind your own business," Carlos said.

Katía sat back and studied the shore. *I wonder if I will ever meet the right person.* The sight of the house snapped her out of her thoughts. "That's it!"

Carlos looped the boat around and pulled back even with the house. The moonlight produced a soft glow while yellow light poured from the windows.

"This is perfect," Katía said, binoculars trained. "I see two of the guys. They're all the way at the front of the house… on a couch… maybe watching TV. Where is that girl?"

She continued searching, checking each window carefully. "I don't see her anywhere."

"Maybe she's their sister and already in bed," Carlos said. "It is getting late for farmers."

"She could have been a date who doesn't live there," Luna added.

Katía continued scanning what she could see through the windows. "I just have a bad feeling about this. What if they're holding her as a sex slave?"

"That would be horrible," Luna said. "But what can we do? We don't even see a girl tonight. I think it's time to go home and see if we can come up with any other ideas."

Katía checked her watch, which read 10:34. "You're right. I do have to preach tomorrow."

The park pals gathered around Katía's car while Carlos pulled the boat out of the water.

"We didn't see the girl, but I still have a hunch that she's there," Katía explained to Fitz and Zee. She patted Fitz on the back. "Are you shaken up after the dogs nearly got you?"

"I'm OK," Fitz said.

"Should we call the police and tell them what we suspect?" Luna asked.

"They won't be able to check it out," Fitz answered. "Just because we saw a girl there doesn't give them probable cause to get a warrant."

Forming a grin, Katía said, "I know what we have to do. Divide and Conquer, Phase Two."

CHAPTER 9

At 5:00 p.m., the park pals met at the boat ramp on Sunday afternoon. The sun had pounded the asphalt all day, and it still responded by throwing back searing heat.

"I don't see how you guys survive in this heat," Luna said to Fitz and Zee.

"Summers ain't easy," Zee replied.

"I still think this is a bad idea," Fitz said. "I don't want to go to jail."

"Well, you go on the boat and I'll go with Katía," Zee said. "I have to do everythin' I can to get that girl back to her family. And besides, jail has AC."

Fitz rolled his eyes. "You realize that not all of Katía's hunches can be right."

"She was right about Crystal," Luna added, hands going to hips.

"I'm not discounting Katía's intuition, but this is a crazy idea," Fitz replied.

"I'm open to any better ideas," Katía said, hands on her hips, too.

Fitz threw up his hands. "I sure hope I don't have to say, 'I told you so.'"

Katía huffed and wondered if Fitz was right. *I hope he's wrong.* "Zee and I'll wait here till you call and say you're near the house, then we'll take off. If something goes wrong, text me."

"Got it," Luna said.

"No, I'm going with Katía. I want to be there in case something does go wrong," Fitz said.

"My knight in shining armor," Katía chuckled, patting him on the shoulder.

"I can handle it," Zee protested.

"Yeah, but you can't run if you need to."

"I'm almost as fast as you."

"Guys, hush. Let's just go with the original plan of Fitz and me going to the house. Zee, I think we need your gift of gab to help keep them down by the lake."

"OK, but you'd better get that girl out of there if you find 'er," Zee said.

"Great. Let's launch Operation Divide and Conquer, Phase Two," Katía replied.

While they were talking, Carlos had launched the boat, tied it to the dock, and parked the 4Runner. "I'm ready whenever you are," he said, walking up to the group.

"Sorry I was busy talking and didn't help," Luna said.

"No problem. Are you guys sure this is a good idea? We're going to be trespassing."

"I didn't see any 'No Trespassing' signs," Luna said.

"OK, then. Let's get moving."

Carlos slowed the boat and aimed it toward the place where he wanted to beach it, but a cow was in the way.

"This is the only spot safe enough to beach the boat," he said.

"Keep goin' real slow. She'll move," Zee replied.

As Carlos continued on the path toward the cow, the cow mooed, then sauntered out of the water.

"All right, let's see how long it takes them to notice us," Luna said.

Luna and Carlos climbed down the ladder, and Zee handed them a few pieces of firewood. They hauled the wood to the fire ring, which was already set up about ten feet from the shore.

Luna called Katía. "We're here. I'll let you know when we get their attention."

Carlos returned to the boat, and Zee handed down a picnic basket.

"What if they don't come out?" Carlos asked as he set the basket down near the fire ring. "They could be watching a preseason football game and never notice us."

"I'll make sure they notice," Luna said. "You might have to cover your ears. … Wait, let's try this first. Zee, turn the radio up loud."

Zee reached for the radio, then jumped at the report of a shotgun.

Luna was still connected to Katía. "I guess you heard that. They want to make sure we leave. Hold on, only two of them are coming. Aren't there three brothers?"

"I think so," Katía said. "I hope there are no parents around."

"I don't think you're going to get the chance to find out," Luna said. "I still don't see the third guy."

The man with the shotgun continued marching toward them, with the shorter one trailing just behind and off to the side.

"Do you have a gun, Zee?" Carlos asked while they were still a good way off.

"Yeah, but I didn't think to bring it with me."

"Great. Should we put up our hands?" Carlos asked.

Luna said, "Just leave it to me. Katía, I need to hang up. I assume the third one is still in the house."

Luna picked up the basket and took a few steps toward the man with the shotgun. "I apologize if this is your property. We saw the fire ring the other day and thought it would be a nice place to picnic."

"Get off our land," the man grumped.

"That's exactly what we're doing," Luna replied. "I hope you have a good evening. You do have a beautiful place here."

She and Carlos left the firewood and waded back to the boat. The two men stood in threatening stances, shotgun forward but aimed at the ground. Carlos backed the boat away from the shore and headed back to the boat ramp. Zee waved as they left the farm.

"He didn't wave back," Zee said, oozing disappointment.

Luna called Katía and reported what had happened. After she disconnected, Katía slammed her fist onto her knee. "That didn't go as planned."

"No, but at least everyone is OK," Fitz answered.

Katía pulled her Prius off the side of the road, where she had parked near the driveway, and headed to meet the others at the boat ramp.

"I wish we could see the house from the road," Katía said. She went silent for a moment. "Don't tell the others, but I'm coming back with my camera after dark."

"Oh, no," Fitz said "Is there any way I can talk you out of that? They greeted the others with a warning from the shotgun. I don't think they'll use a warning shot if they catch you prowling around at night."

"You don't have to come," she said, wishing she hadn't. *I really don't want to do this by myself.*

"Yes, I do. I can't let you do something crazy alone." He fished out some M&Ms.

Back at the boat ramp, Katía held out her hand to Carlos. "Thank you so much for your help."

"You're absolutely welcome. Now I see why Luna gets into so much trouble with you folks," Carlos said with a chuckle. "Seriously though, I think you need to leave those guys alone. They're dangerous."

CHAPTER 10

Fitz pulled into the parking lot at the boat ramp on Lula Road at 8:00 p.m. sharp. It was usually a deserted place, but today, a lone pickup truck was backed into the far corner. The sunlight had faded to a dull gray. Fitz ignored the truck and got out his PocketRocket camp stove and a can of Beanee Weenees.

He stripped off the paper and opened the can. While he was lighting the little stove, he heard footsteps. Looking up, he saw a man approaching from the truck. *Oh, no. I left my gun in the car.*

"Good evening," the man said with a smile. He was tall, thin, and brown-haired.

"Hey," Fitz said curtly, hoping the man would go away.

"I haven't seen you here before. My name's Dan."

"Hey," Fitz said again, adjusting the flame and setting the can on it to heat.

"You're cooking supper. That's a nice setup."

This guy is going to be chatty. "Thanks."

"Are you looking to hook up for the night?" Dan asked.

Fitz looked up at him, trying to keep irritation from registering on his face. "No, I'm not," he managed. He got up and put the harness on Buffett and let him out, then he walked around the car and stealthily pulled out his Beretta. Sliding it into his waistband, he hoped the guy didn't notice.

"That's a pretty cat. What's its name?"

"Buffett." He got a pot holder and spoon and stirred the Beanee Weenees.

"It was a hot one today, wasn't it?" the guy asked.

Fitz's patience was done. "Look, I just want to eat my supper in peace."

Dan held up his hands in surrender. "OK. I get it. I was just trying to be friendly. Jeez."

Fitz opened his mouth, almost responding with, "Sorry," but he held it in, fearing that response would spur the guy on. Dan walked back to his truck and left.

The sun had set, and Fitz turned on his headlamp to see what he was doing. Just as he was finishing supper, Katía pulled into the lot. "Whatchya doing?" she asked.

"Just cleaning up supper," he replied. *I was hoping to finish before she got here.*

"That's a meager supper," she said, eyeing the empty can. "Do you think it'll give you enough energy for our mission tonight?"

"It'll do. I still think this is a bad idea."

"It's not like that old house is equipped with the latest security. They'll never even know we were there."

"It could use a coat of paint, but that doesn't mean they haven't installed video surveillance."

"Did you notice any cameras the first time we went?" Katía asked.

"No."

"Me, either. So quit worrying, and let's go."

Fitz tugged his beard a few times. "Do you have your gun?"

"Of course. I don't go anywhere without it anymore."

After Fitz hesitated, Katía added, "Bring Buffett."

Katía parked her Prius along the side of the road just down from the driveway.

"I hope they don't have dogs. Can you turn off the interior lights so they won't shine when we open the doors?" Fitz asked.

"Probably, but I don't know how." Without hesitation, she opened the door.

As he got out, Fitz said, "Close the door quietly."

"I wasn't planning to slam it," Katía huffed. She looped the camera strap around her neck and donned a shoulder holster. "Ready."

They walked down the winding driveway till they could see lights through the trees. Fitz stopped and studied what he could see of the house. Something wasn't right.

As Katía started to move forward, Fitz put out an arm to stop her.

"What?" she whispered.

Fitz kept his eyes on the front porch. He saw what had barely registered earlier: the red light from a cigarette. "Someone's on the porch," he whispered, his arm still held out. "Stay still."

"You're the one we have to worry about with your white, shiny face," Katía whispered. She was dressed in black. She aimed her camera at the window, zoomed in through the tree limbs, and studied the screen.

"I see two of the guys sitting on the couch. I think they're watching TV."

Fitz put his finger to his lips, and Katía nodded. He saw the red light fly to the ground, then the door opened, and the guy went back inside.

"If you didn't see the girl, I think we should go," Fitz whispered.

"Not yet. Let's get a little closer. It's hard to see through these trees." She moved toward the house without waiting for Fitz's response.

He followed, tripping on a root and stumbling into Katía before regaining his balance. She put her finger to her lips. In the moonlight, Fitz could see she was grinning.

They stopped at the point where there were no more trees blocking the house. Katía aimed the camera and focused. Fitz noticed when her spine stiffened.

"What?" he asked.

"It's the girl. She's walking into the den with one of the guys behind her." She gasped, snapping a photo. "There's a rope around her waist, and he's holding onto the end of it!" She snapped three photos.

"Is she trying to get away?"

"It doesn't look like it. She sat down in a recliner, and he sat down near her on the couch. He's still holding the rope."

"That's odd," Fitz mused. Remembering Dan's offer from earlier he wondered, "Maybe they're into some kind of weird sex stuff."

Katía smacked him on the shoulder. "How could you think something like that? She's obviously a hostage."

"Can you tell if it's Sadie?"

"I've only seen the side of her face, but it could be her."

"It also could not be her." Fitz replied, trying to give himself a reason not to storm the house.

"There's only one way to find out." Katía followed the pasture fence to the side of the house for a head-on look at the girl.

Fitz followed, pulling out the Beretta on the way. *I wish I could stop her.* He wanted to catch up, grab her arm, and pull her back to the car, but he was afraid her protest would gain the men's attention. Instead, he followed till they were next to the house.

Katía motioned for Fitz to stay put. She walked about twenty feet away from the house, then moved to see into the window. Fitz saw her hand go to her mouth before she pulled up the camera.

After a brief pause, Katía hurried back to Fitz. Getting close to his ear, she whispered, "It's Sadie." She held up the camera to show Fitz.

He whispered into her ear, "We need to get to the car and call the sheriff's office."

Fitz had taken five steps away from the house when he heard the front door open. He froze. Katía sneaked back close to the side of the house. She motioned for Fitz to join her.

Fitz fox walked to the side of the house, got between Katía and the corner of the house, then aimed his gun. Hearing what sounded like someone sitting down in one of the rocking chairs, he let out a slow breath. *Smoking again?*

An interminable wait led to the sound of the door opening and closing again. Fitz motioned for Katía to go, and she led the way.

Back inside the car, Fitz pulled up the photo of the missing Sadie Langston so they could compare it to the girl in Katía's photo. He leaned over and studied the two images with her. When their shoulders touched, Fitz pulled back.

"I don't have cooties, you know," Katía laughed.

Fitz couldn't think of anything to say, so he just popped a few M&Ms into his mouth and studied the photos. "This does look like the same girl. It's odd that there are no bruises or other signs of abuse."

"She doesn't look happy, though. I don't think she's there by choice."

"I'll call it in."

"It might be better if I called it in. They seem to have issues with you," Katía grinned. "Pull up the address on your map." She dialed 911.

When the dispatcher answered, Katía explained that they had found Sadie Langston and gave the address.

The dispatcher asked, "How do you know it's the missing girl?"

"I have the photo from her missing person report, and I have a photo of the girl we just saw. They're the same."

"I'll get a deputy on the way. He'll want to see the photo before going to the house."

"Sure. We're parked on the side of the road near the driveway in a Prius."

CHAPTER 11

Fitz and Katía sat in the darkness, waiting for the deputy to arrive.

"It looks like your hunch was right again," Fitz said. "The sheriff's department will want to bring you on as a consultant."

Katía laughed. "I doubt it, but I am glad we found this girl and that she looks to be OK."

"Yeah. I'm sure her parents will be relieved to have her back."

"Oh! We need to let the others know, especially Zee." She sent a group text explaining how they had found Sadie, even attaching a photo since her phone could connect to the camera via Bluetooth.

The phone immediately pinged with three celebratory responses. Zee added, "I wish you'd let me know. I'd love to have been there."

It took about fifteen minutes before they saw car lights approaching from behind. The car slowed, blue lights began to flash, and the deputy pulled in behind them.

"Leave your gun in the car, and let's get out," Fitz said. "But bring the camera."

"Yes, sir," Katía replied.

They stood, and the deputy ordered them to stay put. Shining a flashlight, he walked up and introduced himself as Deputy Morgan. "I understand you have information regarding a missing teenager."

"Yes, sir. We found her at this house. We have photos so you can see that they match." She held out her camera, and Fitz held out his phone.

"You say she's at the house that this driveway leads to?"

"Yes," Katía replied.

"I'm not going to ask how you got this photo, but I am going to ask how long it's been since you took it."

"About twenty-five minutes," Fitz added.

Deputy Morgan aimed his flashlight at Fitz. "Fitz Fitzgerald. You always seem to be around when something questionable happens."

"The only questionable thing here is the kidnapping of that girl," Fitz replied.

"I'll agree that is the *most* questionable thing. Anyway, you probably know the drill. I need to get that photo sent in so I can request a search warrant. Then I'll approach the house. In the meantime, I need the two of you to leave."

"You mean you're not going to rescue her now? She's sitting in the living room. What if the men do something horrible while you're just standing here waiting?" Katía fumed.

"Ma'am, we have laws in this country, and I have to obey them. It's time for you to leave," Deputy Morgan said firmly.

"Thanks, deputy. I appreciate your service," Fitz said, then got into the car.

Katía got in with a huff, then drove back to Fitz's car at the boat ramp. "I can't stand not knowing if they rescue her. What if they get away while he's waiting for the warrant? What if they decide to rape her before he gets there?"

"Calm down," Fitz said. "The deputy has to wait for the warrant, or he can't legally enter the house. If he knocked on the door without a warrant, all the guys would have to do is say she's not there, then disappear after he leaves. We can find out what happened in the tomorrow."

The next morning, Fitz washed up in the bathroom at Laurel Park. *I wish they had showers here. I sure could use one.* He was scooping Buffett's litter when Zee rolled in.

"Hey, man! It's a glorious mornin', as Katía would say. I'm so happy you got that girl rescued. Last night was the first time I slept good since I heard she was missin'."

With a smile, Fitz said, "You're on a roll this morning."

"Yeah. There's nothin' like a clear conscience."

The lights of three cars bumped over the speed hump at the top of the hill.

"You'd better hurry," Fitz said.

"Don't leave without me." Zee hurried into the bathroom to wash up.

Katía, Ben, and Luna parked, and Katía hurried out of her car.

"It's a glorious morning! Hey, everybody," Katía said, proceeding to hug everyone in the group. "I'm so happy Sadie is safe and will be reunited with her family. God used us in a wonderful way!"

She came to Fitz, and he leaned into the hug, finding he even looked forward to the routine now.

"You sound just like Zee. He was all excited, too," Fitz said. "I sure hope it was the right girl and they were able to rescue her."

Katía stopped, spine stiffening. "What do you mean?"

Fitz held up his hands at her aggressive stance. "I just mean it's possible something could have gone wrong. It could have been a girl that looks a lot like Sadie, or they might have noticed the blue lights and taken off before the deputies got there."

"Or they might not have issued a warrant," Ben added.

Katía's hands went to her hips. "Y'all really know how to crush a gal."

Zee popped out of the bathroom. "There's another hero!" He hurried over to hug Katía.

"Fitz just threw cold water on our excitement," Katía said.

"Yeah, I heard. But the possibility that she's been rescued is greater than the possibility that she wasn't. I'm gonna claim this is a glorious day until I learn otherwise."

"That's a good philosophy, Zee," Luna added. "It's a happier soul who looks on the bright side."

With Buffett, Snickers, and King leashed up, the park pals started their walk along the trail. The gray, breezy dawn promised the possibility of rain from a hurricane that was crossing the southern part of Georgia and northern Florida.

Katía had her camera but walked with the group instead of stopping to take pictures. "Do you really think there's a possibility that wasn't the right girl?" she asked.

"Let's see the photos you took last night," Ben said.

They stopped while she pulled up the photos and passed the camera around.

Ben pulled up the photo of Sadie Langston and compared them. "It sure looks like her to me. You know, we could ease everyone's worries if Fitz just called and checked on what happened last night."

"Why me?" Fitz asked.

"Because you and Geraldine have a thing going on," Ben chuckled.

"All right," Fitz grumped. He dialed the sheriff's office from memory and asked for Geraldine.

"Hey, Geraldine."

"If it's not my favorite troublemaker. Hey, Fitz, what kind of jam are you in now?"

"I can't imagine why you'd say that," Fitz laughed. "Anyway, I'm not in a jam. I'm calling to find out if they were able to reunite the abducted girl with her family."

"What abducted girl?"

"We called in a report last night about finding Sadie Langston."

"Oh, I see it. When they went in, no girl was there. They're mighty miffed about your call."

"What do you mean there was no girl there? We took photos of her just minutes before we called it in."

"All I can tell you is that a search warrant was issued, the deputies searched the house, and no girl was there."

"I can't believe that. Thanks, Geraldine."

"You're welcome. And try to behave yourself for a change."

Fitz disconnected the call as four concerned faces looked his way. "I guess you figured out that they didn't find her. She said there was no girl there when the deputies searched the house."

"Did they search the barn? They could've hidden her there," Zee said.

"I'm sure they included the barn in their search. That would be the normal procedure," Fitz answered.

"But you don't know for sure," Zee replied. "They could've just asked the guys if she was there and left."

"I don't think they would do that, Zee. Even if they were on the lazy side, I don't know of any officer who wouldn't go the extra mile if they thought a teenaged girl had been abducted."

"Well, I'm goin' back," Zee said, starting to pace.

"What are you going to do? Just walk up to the door and tell them you've come to take the girl?" Fitz chided.

"Somethin' like that."

"Remember, they're armed, at least with a shotgun," Luna added.

"I'll be armed, too," Zee said.

Katía put her hand on Zee's shoulder. "I want to rescue her, too. We need to plan this out to keep everyone safe, though."

"Is there any chance the deputies would go back and do a second search?" Ben asked. "They might catch them off guard."

"They would have to have a reason that justified a new search warrant. They can't just show up willy-nilly," Fitz said.

"OK, then. What's our next step? Try to get more photos to show she's still there?" Katía asked.

Zee went back to pacing. Fitz tugged on his beard. Ben scratched his head and turned toward the lake. Luna put her hands on her hips. Katía studied her camera. Seconds ticked by in slow motion as the park pals searched their minds for a solution.

Fitz was about to give up when Zee said, "I have an idea!"

CHAPTER 12

Fitz looked to Zee, wondering what kind of solution he had come up with to save Sadie. *This should be interesting.* They had to step aside on the park trail to let a jogger pass before Zee could explain.

"We have to get 'em out of the house somehow. Then we go in and get her. I say we start a fire on their property away from the house. When they go to put it out, we sneak in and get the girl." Zee looked expectantly at the others.

"Other than risking burning down the whole county, that could work," Fitz snarked.

"I like the idea of coming up with a way to get the guys out of the house, but I'm not too fond of fire, especially with how hot and dry it is." Katía said.

"It's s'posed to rain today," Zee added with a grin. "It's divine timing."

"What if their cows got out and were wandering down the road?" Ben asked.

"They're fenced in. They can't get out," Luna said.

"They can if someone cuts the fence and just happens to lay a trail of apples," Ben grinned.

"Ben, you're brilliant. That's even better than fire," Zee said.

"Other than the minor detail of destroying private property, that has potential," Fitz added.

Katía said, "There is a major problem. If I had an abducted girl in my house, I'd keep one person there to guard her and only send two out to tend to the cows."

"That's a good point," Fitz said.

"One's better than three. Let's go," Zee said, starting toward the cars.

"Hold on, Zee," Fitz called. "I think we have a few more details to work out."

"How about a double distraction?" Luna said.

"OK, what's a double distraction?" Fitz asked, tugging his beard. Buffett rubbed his legs, winding between them and tangling him in the leash. "Must you? Can't you see we're talking about something important here?" Fitz worked his legs free while Luna explained.

"If we can get two of them to leave for the cows, one of us can knock on the front door with a long, sad story about a flat tire while the others slip in through the back door to find the girl," Luna explained.

"And just what makes you think the back door will be unlocked?" Fitz asked, sounding testier than he had intended. "If they're holding Sadie against her will, then they will be on high alert for intruders."

Fitz watched as everyone deflated. *OK, I have to come up with some way to save that girl.*

Ben blurted out, "What if the girl we saw is their sister?"

Four pairs of eyes glared at him like he was a three-eyed goat.

"Ben, didn't you see the picture? That girl is Sadie Langston, no doubt about it," Katía replied. The others nodded.

"OK, you're right. She looks like Sadie," Ben caved.

Silence, the kind that is tense and heavy, weighed down after Ben's comment. Fitz shifted on his feet, pulled out some M&Ms, then looked down at Buffett to try to escape the tension. He bent down and rubbed along Buffett's back. That's when an idea struck.

Straightening back up, he dialed the sheriff's office while saying, "I wonder if they found all three men there."

When Geraldine answered, Fitz asked, "Did the deputies find three men in the house they searched last night?"

"I'm afraid to ask, but why do you want to know that?" Geraldine replied.

"It'll let me know if one of them took the girl and hid her."

"I don't like where this is going, Fitz."

"Just satisfy my curiosity," Fitz pleaded.

After a beat of hesitation, Geraldine replied, "Give me a minute to pull up the report. … It says two males, ages eighteen and twenty-two, were in the house at the time of the search."

"Thanks, Geraldine. You're a peach."

"Now don't go getting into trouble with that information. You stay out of this."

"You know me better than that."

"That's what I'm worried about."

Fitz disconnected the call and explained his theory. "They only found two of the men in the house when they searched. I'm betting the third one took the girl and hid out in the woods."

"Or under the house," Katía added.

"That's just gross. What if they're makin' the poor girl live under the house?" Zee fumed. "Let's go. We cain't wait any longer."

"It would be better if we wait till dark," Fitz said. He got the same three-eyed goat look they had given Ben.

"You can stay here if you'd rather," Zee said.

"Good grief," Fitz responded. "I suppose you still have your cut-off tool in the car." He looked to Ben.

"Of course, but I think we need a broken post to make it look more realistic," Ben answered. "That'll take a saw or an ax. If we're going to do this, it's probably best to go in one car. It'll draw less attention. Zee and I'll manage the fence and report the cows are out, Luna can do the flat tire drama, and Katía and Fitz can check under the house. Does that sound like a plan?"

"I'd rather storm the house than mess with the cows," Zee said.

"I think we need the fleet of foot folks to go to the house just in case," Ben replied.

After placing the pets in the house and retrieving an ax and a bow saw, Ben dropped Luna, Fitz, and Katía off on the side of road. He and Zee proceeded past the driveway to open the fence and lure the cows out with a bag of apples.

Fitz, Katía, and Luna crossed the ditch and entered the woods. Katía stopped and pulled bug spray from her purse and sprayed her pants cuffs, socks, and shoes. "Anyone else care for some?"

"Sure," Luna said.

Fitz shook his head and studied the woods to find the best path that would lead them to the back of the house.

"OK, you know what to do, right?" Fitz asked when Luna handed the spray back to Katía.

"Yep. I wait till Ben leads the guys out to the cows. If only two of them go out, then I go knock on the door. I think I'll tell them I'm lost instead of having a flat tire since I don't have a car."

"OK," Fitz replied. "Got your gun?" he asked Katía.

"Yep," she patted her purse.

Fitz started to ask why she was carrying a purse, then thought it would be better left unsaid. He led the way through the woods, side-stepping briars and holding limbs to keep them from flipping back and slapping Katía.

Reaching a point from which he could see the back of the house through the trees but was still sufficiently hidden, Fitz stopped.

Katía wasn't watching and bumped into him. Fitz reached back instinctively to steady her, his hand landing on her hip. "Sorry," she whispered.

He removed his hand quickly, face flushing.

"Are you blushing?" Katía whispered.

"No." He turned his attention toward the house, watching for Ben.

While they waited, Katía pulled binoculars from her purse and studied the windows. There were four windows on that side. She whispered, "The first three are covered with sheers, and the lights are off. I can't tell if anyone is in the rooms. The window in the back is the kitchen, but I don't see anyone in there, either. There aren't any lights on."

"No one's in the garden, either."

"Maybe they're late sleepers," Katía said.

"If so, they won't be happy when Ben knocks on the door," Fitz chuckled.

Katía scanned the barn, not seeing any activity there, either. A few minutes later, Ben walked down the driveway. Fitz heard the knock and waited. He heard another knock.

"These guys must be heavy sleepers," Fitz whispered.

"Or they're gone," Katía whispered back.

Ben appeared around the corner of the house, shrugged his shoulders, then proceeded to the back. He looked toward the garden, then knocked on the back door. Fitz relaxed his clenched fist as he waited for the door to open. When nothing happened, he said, "Let's go."

Fitz walked out of the woods toward Ben, who crossed the yard to meet them.

"It appears no one is home," Ben said.

"Or they're just not answering the door after last night," Fitz replied.

"If that's the case, we don't need to be standing here in the open," Katía said and moved close to the house. She found a hole in the foundation where a vent used to be. Aiming the flashlight on her phone through it, she called, "Is anyone in there?" She looked and listened, but there was no response.

"If she's under there, she's probably gagged," Fitz said.

"Let's look for another entryway, then," Katía said and rounded the back corner. "Just what I was hoping for."

Fitz heard hinges squeak and rounded the corner just in time to see Katía crawl through the opening. He hurried over and looked inside. Katía stopped and swept her phone side to side, the light revealing dirt and cobwebs.

"I don't believe anyone has been under here in a long time," she said.

"Come on back out," Fitz urged.

Katía stood, then brushed her hands and knees to get some of the dirt off. When she straightened up, Fitz couldn't help staring at her hair.

"What?" Katía asked.

"You've got spiderwebs in your hair," Ben stated.

"Yuck!" She started grabbing at her hair but wasn't succeeding at removing them.

"Here. Be still, and I'll help you," Fitz said.

Katía stopped, leaned forward, and Fitz pulled the webs from her hair.

"Thanks. That was mighty kind of you," she said.

"You're welcome," Fitz said, trying to shake the webs off his fingers. He gave up, bent down, and wiped his hands through the grass till they were web-free.

When he looked up, Katía was climbing the steps to the back door. "What are you doing?"

It was too late. She reached and turned the doorknob. "Locked," she reported. "I'm going to check the front door."

Fitz and Ben followed her to the front, where she found another locked door. "Should we break in?"

"No. I don't have my lock-picking kit anyway," Fitz answered. "We need to let Zee and Luna know what's going on."

Stepping off the porch, He saw Zee and Luna walking down the driveway. "Nobody home?" Zee called.

"Not a soul," Ben answered.

"That's what I figured. The cow's back home and the fence repaired," Zee added.

Fitz tugged his beard. "How'd you fix the fence?"

"Turns out, the wires were already broken and they'd just nailed up a couple of boards. I hammered 'em back in with a rock," Zee explained.

"Last night's search must have spooked them, and they've holed up somewhere else," Ben observed.

"How in the world we gonna find 'em?" Zee groaned.

CHAPTER 13

Fitz rubbed down Buffett's back after parking in the deck next to the library. He checked to make sure all the windows were cracked open.

"I won't stay long. Just need to catch up on some reading," he explained to the cat as he fished a supply of M&Ms out of the Yeti travel mug and loaded the Velcro pouch.

"Meow."

The truth was Fitz needed a break from the heat. The rain expected from the hurricane had not materialized. In fact, the clouds had cleared and the sun was shining with a vengeance.

Goosebumps danced on his arm when he walked through the library doors. It was 3:55 in the afternoon when he sat down at the computer terminal, still reeling from the shock of the cold air.

Fitz checked his watch. *I'll leave by 4:25.* Pulling up the newspaper on the computer, he scanned the headlines. Arrests for child pornography or drugs and new housing developments were the fare for the day. One article did catch his attention.

"Attempted Kidnapping at Bus Stop," the headline read.

"In Denver, South Carolina, a 16-year-old girl escaped an attempted kidnapping while waiting at the bus stop on the morning of August 16."

That's today.

"The girl told police that two men jumped out of a red pickup truck and approached her. She said she told them to leave her alone and backed away while pulling bear spray from her purse.

"She said the men told her they wanted to talk to her about Jesus, but when one grabbed her arm, she sprayed both in the face and ran. She described the men as young with black hair and bushy black beards. If you have any information that would help the police locate these men, please call the number below."

The goosebumps returned when Fitz read the description of the kidnappers. *Could this be our guys? … Probably not. There are tons of young men fitting that description. Besides, we have three of them. I'm glad she got away.*

Fitz kept looking through the paper, but his mind was stuck on the article about the girl. *It was a red pickup, though.* Fitz noticed he was cold and checked his watch. *Time to get back to Buffett. At least he's been in the shade.*

The heat smacked Fitz in the face as if he had hit a wall. *Now I remember why I went inside.* He found Buffett curled up asleep in the passenger seat.

"Hey, buddy. You OK?"

Buffett stood and stretched in a leisurely way.

"It looks like you're fine." He reached over to pet the cat, then Buffett hopped into his lap and purred. Fitz leaned back in the seat. "What shall we do for supper tonight?"

"Meow."

"You're always interested in food. It's too hot to cook, so I think I'll just pick up something."

Fitz couldn't remember how long he had been talking to Buffett that way. The cat didn't seem to mind, especially if the conversation involved something to eat.

Thinking about his supper options, Fitz decided a chicken salad from Zaxby's would hit the spot.

"Is chicken OK with you?"

"Meow."

"Good. A Zaxby's salad it is, then."

Fitz lay his head against the headrest and stroked Buffett's soft fur. The next thing he knew, he was awakened by a passing car.

"I didn't mean to fall asleep." Buffett was curled up in the passenger seat. "Let's go get that chicken salad." He checked his watch which read 5:12. "Let's take it to the park and get a picnic table in the shade. Maybe there will be a breeze."

"Meow."

* * * * *

Katía served her plate with a dinner-cut slice of deli ham, black-eyed peas, and broccoli. She thought about Fitz and Zee as she sat down at the two-seater table in her kitchen. *Lord, please help keep them cool. I wonder how many more people are out there suffering in this heat. Even if they're not homeless, if they don't have air conditioning, they would still be miserable. Lord, thank you for this food. Amen.*

Looking through the kitchen and down the hallway, she felt the emptiness of her home. It was a small, one-story brick home with three bedrooms. *I could let Fitz and Zee stay here. They could each have a room. It's such a waste of space for just me, Snow, and Cotton.*

As if they heard her call them through her thoughts, Snow and Cotton meowed and rubbed her legs, leaving traces of white fur on her navy slacks.

"You know the rules. You'll get your treats as soon as I finish supper." *I'll have to pray about the idea of inviting them to live here. I doubt the congregation would be thrilled with the idea of my shacking up with two guys.*

Katía laughed as she pictured the expressions of a couple of her more sanctimonious members when they heard the news of Fitz and Zee moving in. *That kind of makes me want to go ahead and do it! I wonder if they would accept the invitation.*

Her phone pinged with a notice from the Gainesville Times. She kept a subscription to the local paper to help keep up with community news. After a bite of ham, she opened the phone to see what the hot news alert was.

"Teenage Girl Kidnapped in Toccoa," was the headline. Pulling up the article, she read while she ate.

"A 15-year-old girl was kidnapped in front of her mobile home after getting off the school bus this afternoon. Students on the bus reported seeing a red pickup stop behind the bus. Two men jumped out and dragged the girl into the truck. The bus was too far away for them to get a good look at the men, but they said the men had black hair and beards. The truck color and description of the men match an attempted kidnapping in Denver, South Carolina, earlier today. If you have any information regarding the whereabouts of the girl, please call the Stephens County Sherriff's Department."

There was a picture of the girl with her name, Laurie Jones.

That has to be the same guys. I bet they were out trying to abduct another girl this morning when we were at the house.

Without hesitating, she copied the phone number from the article and called the sheriff's department. She explained what she knew about the guys at the lake house. The lady on the phone thanked her for the information and said she would forward it on.

After disconnecting the call, Katía bowed her head. *Dear God, please keep these girls safe. Let them be rescued before these men do terrible things. Amen.*

She dutifully chopped up some of her ham for Cotton and Snow, put it down on two saucers, then cleaned up her dishes. The clock on the microwave read 7:37 when she was done. She eyed the cookie jar in which she kept assorted dark chocolates but decided her waist would thank her if she abstained.

She picked up her current book, "Thomas Merton: Spiritual Master," and settled into the recliner to read. Snow settled onto her lap while Cotton snuggled up next to her thigh.

Opening the book, she saw the faces of the two missing girls instead of words. The girls' faces faded into memories of her own abduction, and a shiver of terror flowed along her spine. With darkness gathering outside, she knew she couldn't stand staying home. *I have to see if they're at that house. What if the deputies don't come till in the morning? It might be too late!*

Cotton and Snow jumped to the floor as she let the footrest down. After changing into black jeans, a black shirt, and black shoes, she donned the shoulder holster. With camera in hand, she headed toward the men's house.

CHAPTER 14

Katía pulled to the side of the road and took three deep breaths to calm her nerves. She closed her door quietly, slid her phone into her back pocket and started for the house. After five steps, she remembered to silence her phone, then continued on.

She paused at the point the trees no longer blocked her view of the house and peered through the windows. She could see two of the guys sitting in the den. *I wonder where the third one is.*

She followed the fence till she was across from the side wall of the house, then crossed over and hovered close to the house. Her nerves zinged on high alert, and for the first time, she wondered if this had been a wise idea. Hearing the TV on inside, she stepped away from the house and looked through the window. *I still don't see the third guy.*

She moved to get a different angle but still saw only two of the young men. *Maybe he's in the bathroom.* Sounds from the direction of the barn sent a slow burning shock up her spine. She froze, not even daring to breathe, as the sound of footsteps approached. She pulled the screen of her camera screen into her belly, hoping it would block the light. She took in a slow, controlled breath. The footsteps stopped.

The sound of a shotgun cocking was followed by, "Don't move." More steps. The barrel of the gun punched into her back. "Walk to the porch." A shove from the gun urged her forward.

She took stiff steps, her mind scrambling for a way out. *It's dark. I might could draw my Glock and fire before he realizes what's happening. That's a life-or-death gamble, though.* She kept moving forward, fearing that once he got her inside, her life would be over anyway. *If I spin and grab the barrel, would that give me time to pull my gun?* She realized the barrel wasn't touching her anymore. *He's too far away. It's like he sensed what I was thinking.*

His booming voice startled her. "Don't try anything funny. Hey, Earnie! Open the door. I found somethin' worse than a coyote."

"Don't tell me ya done brought in a skunk."

"Naw. It's a intruder."

"Whatchya talkin' 'bout?" The screen door opened, and the young man Katía had seen the first time she and Fitz had come stepped onto the porch. "Great cow cud! Whatchya doin' lurkin' around in the dark?"

Katía went with the only thought that had come while she listened to their exchange. "I got lost."

"You got lost. Anyone in they right mind would've come to the door 'stead a lookin' through the winder," the one with the shotgun said. "She wuz a-spyin' on us."

"Spyin', huh? Don't sound like you wuz lost to me. Brang her on in, Earl."

Earl complied with a shove from the shotgun, and Katía climbed the four steps to the porch, every fiber of her being dreading stepping through that door.

"I'm sorry I've bothered you. I didn't mean to get lost and end up here. If you don't mind, I'll just be on my way and see if I can get back to the car," Katía pleaded.

The third young man appeared near the door. "She got a gun, Earnie!"

"Good eye, Everett. Ma'am, we don't take kindly to intruders with guns. Raise yer arms, and I'll relieve ya of it."

Katía's arms felt like lead. She wanted to grab the Glock and start shooting. She wanted to scream and run and hope they wouldn't shoot. From somewhere, the still, quiet voice she had learned to heed over the years lightened her arms and told her to comply.

"Thank ya. This'll be a nice addition to our collection," Earnie said as he reached in and removed the Glock from her holster. "Now get inside."

Earl gave her another push, and she walked through the door. *OK, Lord. I don't know why you want me to do this, though.*

The three young men, all with black hair, bushy beards, and hazel eyes hovered around her. Noting their sizes and appearance, she decided they were definitely brothers and that Earnie was the oldest. He was tall, thin, and muscular. The other two were a bit shorter and stockier. It was harder to tell, but she guessed the one with the shotgun was the middle one, and the one called Everett was the youngest.

"I'll take that camera and phone, too" Earnie said. She handed them over.

"Ya think we got another un?" the youngest of the three, whom they called Everett, asked.

"You can have 'er if'n you want 'er," Earnie replied.

"Naw. She's too old for me." Everett said.

"Too old for me, too," Earl, the middle of the three brothers, added.

"What we gonna do with 'er? Everett asked.

"I dunno," Earnie said. "She ain't got no right sneakin' round here at night. She already been here once, knockin' on the door and sayin' she's lookin' for a missin' girl."

"I reckon we should call the police and turn 'er in fer trespassin'," Earl said.

Earnie's eyes darkened, and he cut quick glances at his brothers. "We cain't be doin' that, can we? For now we'll run 'er up in the attic. Pull down the ladder, Everett."

Everett pulled down the folding stairs. Earnie shook the shotgun in that direction. As Katía began climbing, heat washed over her face.

"It's too hot up here. I'll be dead by morning," she pleaded. Looks of surprise erupted on all three of the men's faces, followed by knowing glances.

"It's a test by fire. If ya survive, we'll let ya go," Earnie said. Earl nodded his head. Katía noticed a look of fear wash over Everett's eyes.

Katía stopped climbing, her feet refusing to move.

"Go on. Ya shouldn't have been snoopin' round to start with. If the good Lord wants ya alive, I reckon you'll survive," Earnie prompted.

If the good Lord wants me alive … Lord, I hope you do want me to survive. Please be with me like you were with Shadrach, Meshach, and Abednego in the furnace. A calmness slowed her racing heart, and she climbed on up. "My life is in your hands. You'll have to deal with the guilt if you kill me. … not to mention life in prison," she said just before they lifted the stairs and left her in sweltering darkness.

As Katía worked to squelch the rising panic, a possible escape plan struck. Apparently Earl had the same idea. She heard his voice from below.

"All she's gotta do is push the ladder back down."

"Good thinkin'. I'm gonna screw it in."

That sounded like Earnie. Hope drained from her heart at the sound of a drill locking her in with three screws. She straightened from leaning over and looked around without moving her feet. Faint moonlight trickled in through the gable vents.

Not knowing if there was flooring or just joists around her, she knelt and felt. Plywood surrounded her, so she sat and wiped the first bead of sweat that ran down her forehead. "The only thing I know to do is pray. I can't believe I said that out loud."

"Who's she talkin' to?" Katía heard through the ceiling.

I might as well pray out loud, too. She bowed her head and prayed, "Dear loving God, you created me and said you would always be with me. I pray you'll come and sit with me in this dark time. Please shield me from this heat and help me survive the night."

Words seeped through the ceiling. "Sounds like she's prayin'. Mama taught us killin's wrong. We cain't let her die in the attic … 'specially if she's talkin' to God."

I think that's Everett's voice. You keep talking, and I'll keep praying.

"Shut up, Everett. What other choice do we have?"

CHAPTER 15

A rosy glow in the east promised a beautiful morning. Fitz dropped the bag he had used when scooping Buffett's litter into the trashcan. Returning to the car, he said, "Are the others late, or are we early this morning?"

Buffett looked at the harness.

"I see. You're ready to get out of this car and go for a walk."

"Meow."

"OK. Let's get you suited up, then we'll wait at a picnic table."

By the time he got the harness on Buffett, Zee pulled up. "Mornin'," he said amid groans as he got out of the car.

"Good morning. You must have needed some extra beauty sleep last night."

"You mean it shows already?" Zee grinned.

Buffett hopped out of the Highlander and sauntered over to Zee, rubbing his leg.

"Mornin', Buffett. Here's your treat." He deposited a few cat treats on the asphalt, and Buffett leisurely ate them. "He knows how to savor a treat."

"I'll watch King while you clean up," Fitz offered.

"I'm sure he'd be grateful." Zee leashed up King and handed him a biscuit. "Behave yourself."

Zee entered the bathroom, and Fitz led the two pets to the nearest picnic table. Before he sat down, two more cars came rolling toward him.

"There are Ben and Luna. Katía should be close behind," Fitz said to the cat and the dog.

"Hey, Fitz. You babysitting this morning?" Ben asked as he walked over to the picnic table.

"Yeah. The pay's not much, though."

Luna hurried over. "Good morning! It's a beautiful day. I bet Katía will get some nice shots.

After a glance at the sky, Ben said, "Did you guys see the paper yesterday? There was a story about an attempted kidnapping of a girl in South Carolina."

"Yeah, I saw that," Fitz said. "The description sounded like it could be the guys at that house."

"What?" Luna gasped.

"Let me show you," Ben said as he pulled up the article.

Luna scanned the article, then put her hand to her mouth. "That was yesterday morning! I bet that's where they were when we tried to lure them out."

"I wondered the same thing," Ben said.

Luna kept reading, then noticed a link at the bottom that read, "See related article." She clicked on it and gasped again. "A girl *was* kidnapped in Toccoa. Guess what the guys looked like."

"Black hair and bushy beards?" Ben asked, raising his eyebrows.

Luna nodded and handed the phone back to Ben, her eyes wide. "We have to call the police."

Fitz shook his head. "I don't think that will do any good. They probably won't ask for another search warrant just because we think the descriptions match the guys that live there."

Hands to her hips, Luna said, "It mentioned a red truck. Wasn't there a red truck parked by the barn? That should be a reason to go back."

"It should, but I don't know that it will," Fitz replied.

Luna pulled her phone from a back pocket. "I'm at least going to try. What's the sheriff's number?"

Fitz grunted and called out the number. Luna explained her suspicions to the woman who answered her call, then disconnected.

"She said she would relay the information," Luna said, sounding disappointed. "I was hoping they would hurry out there. Who knows what they're doing to those poor girls."

"Where's Katía?" Ben asked.

"She didn't say anything about not being here today," Luna replied.

"Maybe she went to one of her preacher meetin's," Zee suggested, walking up.

"That's probably it, but she usually tells us," Ben said.

"With all the excitement over the kidnapped girl, she probably just forgot," Luna suggested. "I need to get walking."

The group followed Luna toward the trail. Ben added, "She could have at least texted us this morning."

Fitz opened the little pouch and fished out three M&Ms.

*   *   *   *   *

The night before, when Katía had finished praying in the attic, she opened her eyes. There was no angel, but there was a light. A tiny slit of light seeped through the ceiling about halfway across the attic. *I wonder where that's coming from.*

She felt her way toward the light, stopping when she found something wooden in the way. It was long, and she ran her hands along it. *It feels like a ladder.* She worked her way over it in order to continue on toward the light. *There must be a hole in the ceiling. A light fixture?*

Plywood supported her all the way till she was directly over the light source. The plywood stopped there. Though not continuous, the light appeared to come from a square piece of wood lying on the sheetrock of the ceiling.

Hope grew as she gazed at a potential way out of the attic. *Thank you, Lord. All I have to do is wait for them to go to bed, then I can crawl down from here.*

Sweat dripped from her nose and landed on the wood below. She brushed her hands off on her jeans and pulled up her shirt to wipe her face. *It'll be cooler if I get closer to the vent.*

She started to crawl that way, but the plywood ended. Feeling ahead, she found only joists and a couple of wires. *I've a good mind to see if I can pull this wire loose. Of course, I might just electrocute myself.*

Her attention was captured by voices below. "What if she finds 'em?" It was Everett again.

"Don't matter. She ain't gonna live to tell."

"What if the police come again?"

"We do the same thang we did last time."

"Calm down, Everett. Earnie's got it all figured out. Let's go to bed. We got lotsa work to do tomorrow."

"What if she ain't dead in the mornin'?"

"We'll deal with that then."

Katía was fairly sure the last voice was Earnie's. *He's definitely in charge.* She lay down to wait, hoping it would be a little cooler. Her clothes were now drenched with sweat from the oppressive heat. *They're right. If I don't do something soon, I won't last till the morning.*

She lay on her back, listening to the sounds from downstairs, trying to judge when to explore the light source she had found. Sweat continued to pour. The sounds of creaks from the old house mixed with the hoot of an owl and the flushing of toilets. She counted three flushes. Checking her watch, she decided to wait an hour to give them time to get to sleep.

A voice startled her. "She ain't movin'. Ya reckon she's done dead?"

"Naw. Probably just passed out."

Time crept like a cold sloth. *What if I pass out before the hour's up?* Every time she checked her watch, only a minute had passed. After five minutes, she lifted up enough to see if the light was still coming through the slits. It was.

She decided on a ritual. Every five minutes she would check the light. Each time she found it on, her patience shredded a little more.

After half an hour, she noticed she had stopped sweating. *Uh, oh! I have to do something. I'm getting dehydrated.* A rising panic edged out the patience. *If I faint, I'm a goner.* She decided to go ahead and see what was under that piece of wood. *Lord, please have my back as I try to get out of here. It can't get any worse, can it?*

CHAPTER 16

When Katía rose up to check the light again, she felt dizzy. *This heat is really getting to me.* Her heart skipped a beat when she saw the light still seeping through the crack. She started to lie back down but decided she had to make a move. *If I don't get out of here soon, I'm going to pass out.*

Battling through the dizziness, she began to move toward the light. Nausea decided to join the misery. *It'll serve them right if I throw up.* She crept forward, trying not to make a sound. *Maybe they just leave a light on in the kitchen or something.*

When she finally made it to the light, she felt and located the edges of the wood through which the light seeped. A surge of adrenaline calmed the nausea and dizziness. She braced herself to move the plywood. A sound coming from below froze her in place.

Was that a whisper? Should I lie back down and wait again? I don't think I can stand it.

The whispering floated through the hole again. Katía froze. *That sounds like a girl.* She placed her fingers on opposite sides of the plywood. *Lord, please don't let the guys be down there.* She took a deep breath, blew out slowly, then lifted the board.

Two gasps sounded, and she heard scurrying before she moved the board enough to see through the hole. Realizing she wasn't breathing, she exhaled slowly. She could see the foot of a cot through the opening. No one appeared to be lying on it. Dizziness pressed hard. She waited, expecting the shouting of her captors but heard nothing.

Nerves zinging like a high voltage wire, Katía braced her palms on the flooring beside the opening, bent, and pushed her head through the hole. She saw a blank wall and more of the cot. Hearing movement from the other side of the room, she twisted her head and saw two girls huddled in the corner, faces a blend of terror and curiosity.

She recognized Sadie from the photo. The other girl's face seemed to be covered with black dots. The room began to fade, and her ears rang. The last thing she felt was her shoulders sinking through the hole.

From the blackness, Katía felt something cool touch her forehead. Her mind seemed to turn on slowly, like a computer booting up. She could hear whispers. They sounded concerned. Her tongue felt like cardboard. Finally, consciousness reached her eyes, and she opened them.

Two young, worried faces looked down on her. She was lying on her back. One girl put her finger to her lips, then whispered, "Are you OK?"

Katía's memory seemed to be the last thing to boot up, but she finally remembered where she was. She remembered seeing the girls through the hole in the ceiling. "How did I get here?" she whispered.

"You fell through the ceiling. We caught you and put you on the cot," Sadie explained.

"I think you need some water," the other girl said, holding out a bottle.

Katía sat up. The dizziness resumed, and she leaned against the wall. The girl twisted the top off the water and handed it to Katía. She took a few sips.

"You're the girl from the bus stop, aren't you?" Katía whispered. The girl nodded. "And you're Sadie."

Sadie nodded, then whispered, "How did you know?"

"We found your bottle."

Sadie wrapped her arms around herself and squeezed. A tear slid out of her eye.

Katía drank some more, the water feeling good going down. The only noises were the occasional creaks of the old house and a couple more hoots from the owl. Katía continued to work on getting the water down without drinking it too fast.

Katía surveyed the room. Something was wrong. Three cots and two girls? That wasn't it. A wash of panic zinged her nerves when it dawned on her: "There's not a door."

Sadie shook her head. "The only way out is the hole in the ceiling."

Another question pressed on Katía's heart. She didn't want to ask it, but she had to. "Have they … hurt you?"

Both girls shook their heads.

Katía puzzled over that answer. It didn't make sense. "Why would they keep you prisoner in here and not hurt you … or rape you?"

The girls shrugged their shoulders. Sadie added, "They talk like they're going to kidnap three of us."

"That would explain the three cots," Katía replied. "I don't think one was meant for me."

The girls hovered close to Katía. The girl from the bus stop, blond-haired with dazzling blue eyes, offered her another bottle of water. She took it and asked, "What's your name?"

"I'm Laurie."

"Thank you, Laurie." Katía drank a mouthful of water. "There's no bathroom."

"They let me out to go to the bathroom and even take a shower. Sometimes they have me eat in the kitchen. They always tie a rope around me when they take me out of here," Sadie explained.

"That's what the ladder in the attic is for," Katía realized. "Do they watch when you're in the bathroom?"

"No," Sadie replied. "They do have the window nailed down to make sure I can't get out. I tried."

Sadie looked around, got close to Katía's ear, then whispered, "We were thinking about getting one of us on the other's shoulders to see if we can get into the attic and get the ladder. Now, I'm sure we can do it since there's three of us."

Katía felt a pang of sadness. "I'm afraid they screwed the pull-down stairs closed to make sure I couldn't escape." She watched as both girls seemed to deflate, their shoulders sagging.

"They were just going to let you die up there, weren't they?" Laurie said with a shiver.

Katía looked into her eyes, trying to gauge how to respond. She sensed the girls already knew the answer. "Yes, that's what they said they wanted to do."

"I know!" Sadie said, then covered her mouth realizing she had forgotten to whisper. "There is a vent in the attic. It's big enough for us to get through, if we could pop it out."

"If it's rotten enough, we might could do that without waking the guys," Katía agreed. Her mind started working, weighing the odds of getting caught trying to break out.

She hadn't noticed that the two girls had sat down on the cot right next to her. When she realized that, it dawned on her that they were looking to her for protection and comfort. She wrapped her arms around them, and they snuggled closer.

With as much confidence as she could muster, Katía said, "We're going to get out of here."

She began to think through how to get one of them into the attic. She looked over the two girls and decided Laurie was the lightest, but she sensed Sadie was braver. *I don't think they could get me up there.*

"Do either of you have a flashlight?" Katía asked.

"I keep one in my backpack. I don't think they got it," Laurie replied.

For the first time, Katía noticed two purses and a backpack neatly arranged on one of the cots. *Someone's been organizing.*

"OK. I don't think we can get me up into the attic, and Sadie knows it the best. How would you feel about us lifting you up there?"

Sadie nodded.

"Do you know which side of the house the boys sleep on?"

"The bedrooms are in the back part," Sadie answered.

"Perfect. I want you to be as quiet as you can and go push on the vent that's…" Katía realized she was turned around and didn't know which way the front of the house was.

Sadie seemed to read her mind and pointed. "It's that way."

"Thanks." She checked her watch and was surprised to see it was 1:49. *I was out a long time.*

Laurie fished the flashlight out of her backpack and handed it to Sadie, who turned it on and stuck it into her pocket. Like a colonel, Sadie took charge and positioned Katía and Laurie side by side under the hole. She motioned for Katía to lean over with her hands on her knees like Laurie.

Expecting to have to coach her through it, Katía was amazed when Sadie put one foot on Laurie's thigh, moved the other to her back and was standing with her feet on their shoulders in an instant.

Laurie motioned up, and Katía and Laurie stood with Katía trying to match Laurie's height. Before they were even still, Sadie was through the hole. Laurie held up two crossed fingers, and they waited, listening for groans from the joists.

Katía realized she was holding her breath and exhaled. When she heard Sadie pounding on the vent, she cringed. The noise stopped almost as soon as it began, and they heard Sadie returning.

Her head popped through the hole, and she shook it. "It's solid as a rock."

As Laurie and Katía got into position for Sadie to get down, a voice startled them.

"Earnie, I thank she came back to life. Ya reckon she's a zombie?"

All three of them froze. When they heard no response, Sadie climbed down.

"We're never going to escape," Sadie said when she was back on the floor.

Katía's heart ached as she wiped the tears flowing down Sadie's cheeks. "Never say never. We're going to keep trying till we figure out a way to get away from these guys. We need to come up with another plan, that's all."

"What's going to happen when they come to get us for breakfast?" Sadie said with a tremble.

CHAPTER 17

The park pals, minus Katía, were taking their usual morning walk. As they descended a hill along the trail, Ben suddenly stopped.

"You're brake lights are out," Fitz quipped, putting his hand on Ben's shoulder to prevent a collision.

"Aren't Katía's meetings usually on Mondays?" Ben asked, taking off his hat and running a hand over his head.

"You're right," Luna replied. "You're not thinking what I think you're thinking, are you?"

"Probably," Ben said, looking off in the distance. "She went back to that house last night."

"She wouldn't," Zee said.

"Before we get all worked up, let's call her," Fitz suggested.

"Why didn't we think of that before?" Ben had his phone out and was dialing before he finished that statement.

Fitz's guts had been churning over Katía's not showing. He stared at Ben, trying to will Katía to answer. Finally, Ben spoke, but it was obvious he was talking to her voicemail. Fitz's shoulders tensed, drawing up around his neck.

When Ben disconnected the call, he pushed the phone and both hands into his pockets.

"Oh, no," Zee said.

Fitz tugged his beard. "Let's not overreact. I think we should finish our walk and see if she calls back." He sighed and popped five M&Ms into his mouth.

The park pals completed the loop around the lake in silence. Though no one suggested it, they wound up under the pavilion.

"I'm calling the sheriff's department again," Luna said and placed the call. She explained that Katía was missing and that she suspected she had gone to the house where the girl was being held.

"I'm sorry, ma'am, but an adult who has been missing for less than twenty-four hours is not considered a missing person."

Luna groaned, then shouted, "But she could be in danger along with the two teenage girls. You have to do something!"

The woman on the other end replied, "I'll forward your concern to the deputies, ma'am."

Luna stomped her foot as she disconnected the call. "That is one infuriating woman!"

"I bet she's going to forward the information to the deputies," Fitz said.

"Exactly," Luna replied. "Katía may not have as long as it's going to take for them to do anything."

"Hey, her phone rang four times before it went to voicemail," Ben said.

"So?" Luna asked.

"That means it's on and can be tracked," Ben replied.

"Can you do that?" Zee asked.

"I think so, but it would be a lot quicker if we could convince the sheriff's office to do it," Ben grinned and looked at Fitz.

"What?" Fitz said.

"How about calling to see if Geraldine is working and try to convince her to get them to locate Katía's phone?" Ben said.

Fitz stuck his hands in his pockets and looked off toward the lake. "I hope it wasn't Geraldine that you were just shouting at."

Luna replied, "That might have been her name."

"Great." Fitz pulled out his phone and dialed. "Hey, Geraldine, it's Fitz."

"My favorite problem child. What can I do for you today?"

"I think a friend has been abducted, and I was wondering if you could get someone to locate her phone."

"You sure do stir up a lot of trouble."

"I don't stir it up; it just seems to find me."

"OK, what makes you think she's been abducted?"

After Fitz explained, Geraldine asked, "Is this about the same person that that rude woman just called about? She was shouting at me, you know."

"I know Geraldine, and I apologize for her shouting."

Luna put her hands on her hips.

Fitz continued. "She's worried about our friend. We just called her phone and it was on. Would you please see if they can locate it like right now?"

"Fitz, you're going to get me fired one of these days. Let me see what I can do."

"Thank you so much. I owe you."

"You can say that again, but I doubt I'll ever collect. I'll let you know what they find."

Fitz gave her the number, disconnected the call, and addressed the anxious, waiting friends. "She's going to see if they'll locate the phone."

A collective sigh preceded Ben's comment. "I hope they didn't turn it off after I called."

* * * * *

Katía pondered Sadie's question about what would happen when they came to get the girls for breakfast. She felt her heart speed up while her hands went cold and clammy. "I think they'll be looking for me first. It won't take long to figure out I'm in here. I don't know what they'll do then. I'm sure they won't shoot me here because they couldn't get my body out without a lot of effort."

Wide-eyed, Sadie said, "Do you really think they'll shoot you?"

"I don't know. They were hoping I'd die in the attic, so I'm sure they don't want to let me go."

Silence settled over them. The owl no longer hooted. Katía and the two girls sat on a cot, and the two girls leaned into her. Wrapping her arms around them, she hugged.

"It's a long time till morning. I think we should try to get some sleep," Katía said.

"There's no way I'll be able to go to sleep," Laurie said.

Katía remembered this was Laurie's first night here. She yawned and realized she was exhausted. "I need to lie down for a while. Getting so hot up there took a lot out of me. We can leave the lamp on, if that will help."

"I usually sleep with it on anyway," Sadie replied. "It's too creepy in the dark."

Katía stretched out on one of the cots and closed her eyes. Doubting she would fall asleep, she tried to plan an escape. As she was picturing just running out the door and hoping they wouldn't shoot, she fell asleep and dreamed.

She was in a dark wood. Something was after her. She could hear it walking. Then there was another sound on the other side. Now one behind. She started to run, but they kept pace. "What are you?" she yelled into the darkness. She kept running, face and arms battered by branches. She gave out. "I'm so tired." She stopped and waited for them to attack. A branch broke right behind her, and she startled awake.

"I think you were having a nightmare." It was Sadie. She was rubbing Katía's arm.

"It was awful. I felt so alone."

"I have an idea for us to escape," Sadie whispered.

"Oh?" Katía propped up on an elbow.

"What if we get up in the attic and bang them in the head with the ladder as they come up?"

Katía worked to push the nightmare out of her mind as she considered Sadie's idea. "That has potential, but it also has risks. I think they will come looking for me first and will probably be armed. I would only get one shot. If I miss, I'm dead. Plus, there are two others right behind the first one."

"I'll swing the ladder," Sadie replied firmly. "I don't think they'd shoot me."

Katía patted Sadie's leg. "That's brave. Even if you knock out one of them, what next? They might just leave us here to starve to death."

Sadie's shoulders slumped.

"Look, they're going to want to get rid of me, which probably means two of them will leave to haul me off somewhere. When they're gone, you can try to get away. If they lock you back in here, yell that you have to use the bathroom or, better, say your period is starting. When he lets you out, look for a chance to get away."

"What about Laurie? I can't leave her."

"Sweet talk him into letting you both out. You might have to flatter him or make him think you like him."

"Yuck!"

"It's just an act. You can do it." She patted Sadie's leg again. "What time do they usually come for you?"

"I have no idea. I don't have a watch, and they took my phone."

Katía looked at her watch: 5:07 a.m. "You know what? You said they tie ropes around you when you're out, right?"

"Yeah."

"You and Laurie could run around him in opposite directions until he's wound up. Then untie yourselves and tie him down."

Sadie sat up, shoulders back, and the corners of her mouth turned up just a bit. The beginning smile faded just as fast. "We have to do something before they hurt you or haul you off. I can't bear the thought of that."

I can't bear the thought of that, either, but I don't see any other way. Lord, if you can use my death to save these two girls, then I'm willing.

"What are you thinking?" Sadie whispered.

"To be honest, right now, that seems like the best option for saving any of us. I know they have a shotgun and my pistol. Have you seen any other weapons?"

"I haven't even seen those."

"One more thought. If you get the chance to wind the ropes around one of the brothers, try to get it around his neck and pull hard until he passes out. Your life might depend on that."

"Yes, ma'am."

"Then try to get his phone and call 911. Let's lie back down, and I'll try to think of a plan that doesn't end up with me dying."

CHAPTER 18

The sound of a toilet flushing lurched Katía's nerves into high alert. She sat up so fast that dizziness washed over. The two girls popped up, too. Sadie's wide eyes spoke fear and determination.

Katía called them over and rehearsed the plan. "Sadie's taller, so let her go for the neck while you try to get his arms corralled. If he's smart enough to let go of the rope, do your best to get it around his neck. If that fails, try to knock him over and run."

Laurie's face was wide-eyed and frozen.

"You are brave young ladies. You can do this," Katía said, wrapping her arms around their shoulders. "And don't worry about me. I'm in God's hands, and if God wants to rescue me, it will happen. If not, I'll be in heaven."

As both girls nodded, a voice seeped through the wall. "Everett, how 'bout goin' up and checkin' on that woman, make sho' she's dead?"

"Not me. I think she's a zombie."

"If you thank that, then it's definitely you goin' up. That's the dumbest thang I ever heard."

"Make Earl go. He's older 'n me."

"Great goat's breath. Gimme her pistol so I can go check afore she starts stankin'."

"That was Earl," Sadie whispered. "Looks like he'll be the one to find us. He seems meaner than the other two."

"What if she ain't dead?" sounded through the wall.

"I guess we shoot 'er and plant 'er in the garden," Earnie replied.

The sound of a drill signaled the looming discovery.

"Ready with the gun?" Earnie asked.

"Ready," Earl replied.

"OK, Everett, pull it down."

The springs groaned as the stairs came down. Silence.

"I don't hear no zombie runnin' 'round," Earl said. "I'm goin' up."

They heard him climb, followed by another period of silence.

"Dang, she's gone."

"She done turned into a ghost," Everett croaked.

"She ain't no ghost. Probably just got in the room with the girls," Earnie replied.

"Yep. Looks like the cover's been moved," Earl said.

"Don't shoot 'er in the room. We won't never get 'er out," Earnie said.

The joists creaked, then the ladder began to slide through the hole in the ceiling. "Breakfast time. Come on up," Earl called. "All three of ya," he growled. "I have a gun, so don't try nothin'."

"I'm guessing that's my gun you have. Didn't your mama teach you not to steal?" Katía said, anger lacing her tone.

"Shut up and get up here. It ain't stealin' if yer dead. You come up first, then the nice girls can come up after ya."

Katía nodded to the two girls, then climbed the ladder. Earl stepped back, flashlight and gun leveled at her.

"You just go on down them stairs. Earnie has a shotgun waitin' in case ya get any ideas."

Katía breathed in deeply, then slowly exhaled before walking to meet her fate below. The deadly heat had dissipated overnight, but it was still unpleasant in the attic. She went down the stairs quickly, averse to spending any more time up there.

As she descended the stairs, she heard Earl say, "I hope you two had a nice night. What would you like for breakfast?"

"What I'd like for breakfast is for you to promise not to hurt Katía," Sadie answered from the top of the ladder.

"She done come spyin' on us. We gotta do somethin' about that. It's her fault if she dies."

"That's a bunch of bull. It's on you if she dies. Just picture what your mama is thinking as she's looking down from heaven."

"Did you hear that, Earnie," Everett said. "Mama's watchin' us from heaven. We in trouble."

"Of course she's watching," Katía tried using that leverage. "I'm sure her heart is breaking at the sight of what her boys are doing." Everett wrung his hands and worry etched his face.

Katía watched as Sadie and Laurie came down the stairs behind Earl.

"Don't listen to her. Mama cain't see us, and if she can, she'll understand that we had to do this. We cain't let this woman go tellin' 'bout them girls. Now get them ropes on 'em before they try to get away."

"You do know one of the Ten Commandments is 'Thou shalt not kill," Katía said.

"Mama used to tell us that," Everett squeaked.

Earnie replied, "Yeah, but sometimes it just cain't be helped. People get killed in war, and this is kinda like that."

"Ya really thank we can plant 'er in the garden and nobody'll find out?" Everett asked.

"Yep. The ground's already tilled up. It'll just look like a garden," Earnie replied. "But first, will scrambled eggs be OK for breakfast for you two lovely ladies?"

Everyone flinched at the sound of a phone's ringtone. It was the tune of "How Great Thou Art."

"What in the world is that?" Everett asked.

"I thought I told ya to turn her phone off," Earnie fumed.

Earl replied, "I couldn't figure out how. It kept wantin' a fingerprint."

On the third ring, Katía said, "You should probably let me answer it, or whoever is calling will be worried about me."

Earnie exploded, "Ain't no way you answerin' that phone. I've about had enough of your mouth."

Earl, holding the rope tied around Sadie's waist, said, "Why don't you go ahead and use the bathroom?"

Sadie glared at him, then walked toward the bathroom.

"Y'all know what this means, don't ya?" Earnie said.

"What what means?" Everett asked.

"Since Earl was dumb enough not to turn 'er phone off, somebody can track it and figure out she's here."

"You thank the police are comin' back?" Everett stammered.

Earl stood sentry-like by the bathroom door. "We'd better keep 'em in the room today, then."

"I don't want to stay in that room all day," Sadie shouted from the bathroom.

"I don't reckon we've got a choice, Sadie," Earl replied.

Sadie opened the door and glared at Earl, again. She walked out, and Earl caught hold of the rope trailing behind.

"I might have gotten some pee on the rope. It was in the way," Sadie said.

Earl's eyes widened, and he held the rope with two fingers, wiping his hands on his jeans. "It's wet!"

Sadie sent a grin Katía's way while Everett led Laurie to the bathroom. "Your turn," he said. "Please don't pee on the rope."

Katía was amazed at how kind they sounded when they talked to Sadie or Laurie. *I wonder what they're planning to do to these girls. Are they trying to keep them in good shape to sell them? And why are three young brothers living on this expensive piece of property like they were just country farmers?*

Katía was pulled from her thoughts by Earnie's voice.

"It's worse than that. She got friends might come snoopin' around, too. I thank we got to get out of here if we don't want to lose the girls."

"Whatchya mean, 'Get out of here?'" Earl asked.

"I mean we need to find some place to hide out fer awhile. Give the police time to simmer down and quit lookin' for 'er."

"Where we gonna go?" Everett asked.

"I don't rightly know yet," Earnie said. "Go get that phone. We gotta get it turned off."

Earl tugged on Sadie's rope and pulled her to the den. Again he tried to turn off the phone. "It says it has to have a fingerprint to turn off."

"Well, come get her fingerprint," Earnie called out.

Leading Sadie back into the kitchen, Earl eyed Katía and said, "We gonna do this the easy way or the fun way?"

Katía stuffed her hands into her pockets, stiffened her spine, and glared at Earl.

"That's what I was a hopin'. Everett, hold her still while I borrow her finger. If she fights, I'll just cut it off."

Everett dropped Laurie's rope and grabbed Katía in a bear hug. She dug her hands deeper into her pockets. While Earl tugged, trying to force the right hand out, Sadie and Laurie bolted for the back door.

"They's runnin'," Earnie called. "Catch 'em afore they get away." He leveled the shotgun at Katía.

Laurie crashed into Sadie while Sadie wrestled with the deadbolt. It took her just long enough to get it unlocked that Earl and Everett caught up to them and grabbed the ropes.

"Please don't leave," Everett said.

While Katía was watching the girls being caught, Earnie whacked her in the back with the butt of the shotgun. She jerked her hands from her pockets and caught herself as she hit the floor. Earnie's knee landed on her back, and she was pinned.

"Brang me that phone."

Katía groaned as Earnie wrenched her hand up and held it while unlocking the phone.

"That's how it's done, boys," he said after shutting down the phone.

Earl sneered, "You sure we don't have time to bury 'er afore we leave? She'd make good fertilizer."

CHAPTER 19

After Fitz had convinced Geraldine to get someone to locate Katía's phone, Luna plopped down on the seat of a picnic table. Zee joined her while Ben leaned against the end of the table. Fitz paced. More M&Ms.

"I should have called Geraldine right after Katía didn't answer. It's been too long now. If they have any sense, they would have turned off the phone," Fitz muttered.

"I'm hopin' they don't have any sense, then," Zee said.

"How long do you think it will take?" Luna asked.

Fitz stopped and tugged his beard. "It depends on how busy they are and who's on duty."

"Do you have a guesstimate?" Ben asked.

"It could take five minutes. It could take a couple of hours," Fitz answered.

"A couple of hours!" Luna shouted. "We don't have that long. I think we need to have a look around that house."

"I agree. Let's pay them a visit," Ben replied.

"They're not going to take kindly to us snooping around," Fitz stated.

"I don't take kindly to their snatching Katía. So there," Luna said, placing her hands on her hips. "Is anyone coming with me?"

"I'm goin'," Zee said.

"We definitely need to get there before they hurt her," Ben added.

Fitz looked to the lake. "If they haven't already."

Ben replied, "I can't think of any other reason we couldn't get in touch with her. She knows we expect to see her here at the park."

Fitz tugged his beard. "I'm afraid you're right. Let's go."

"I'll drive," Luna said. "The critters are welcome to come, too."

"I'm taking my Beretta," Fitz said and pulled it out of the car.

They loaded Buffett, King, and Snickers into the back of Luna's 4Runner and took off. On the way, the radio announcer for WDUN, the local station, announced, "Deputies found an abandoned car on Glade Forest Road. It is registered to Katía Bancroft, the pastor of a local church. If you know of her whereabouts, please call the sheriff's office."

"I knew it!" Luna exploded. "They have her. Why did she go back without us?"

No one seemed to have an answer. After stewing for a couple of minutes, Fitz asked, "Ben, how do you want to approach this?"

"I like the direct approach. I'm going to knock on the door, grab the guy by the throat, and not let go till he tells me where Katía is."

"I like it!" Zee said.

Fitz gave his beard another tug. "That should work as long as one of the other brothers doesn't come out with a shotgun."

"He wouldn't risk firing with me so close to his brother," Ben said. "Then I can negotiate a trade. A living brother for a living Katía."

"Don't forget about the other two girls," Luna added. "We need to get them out, too."

"Oh, no. That's her car," Zee said as they approached Katía's Prius, which was parked on the side of the road.

Luna stopped, and Ben hopped out to confirm she wasn't inside. "Not there," he said, getting back into the car.

Luna pulled up in front of the house, and Ben popped open his door before she fully stopped.

"Make sure you shoot them before they shoot me," Ben said as he hurried to the front door.

Fitz jumped out and followed, with Luna and Zee trailing behind. Ben pounded on the door, and Fitz grasped the handle of the Beretta, but left it tucked into his waistband.

Nothing happened. Not a sound came from within the house. Poised with his nose right at the door, Ben pounded again. He looked at the others, then tried the door. "It's locked." He pounded one more time.

"Let's try the back," Fitz said and walked off the porch. The others formed a line behind him. Fitz stopped at the corner of the house and leaned his head around. Seeing no one, he continued.

As Fitz approached the back door, he jumped at the sound of his phone ringing. The others jumped against the side of the house. Fitz tried to figure out how to silence the ring, but since he never got any calls, he couldn't.

He gave up and answered. It was Geraldine, telling him that they had tried to locate Katía's phone, but it was off. Without even looking at the others, Fitz tried the back door, knowing that it would be locked.

"Guys, the truck is gone," Luna said, further confirming their fears that they had taken their hostages and fled.

Fitz shook his head while his heart sank to his knees. He needed no further proof that Katía had been taken captive. *She's gone. I hope she's still alive.*

While Fitz was lost in his sadness, he heard Luna's voice. "I heard the radio story about Katía Bancroft being missing. I know who took her, but I don't know where they are."

She went on to explain about the missing teens, her suspicions that Katía had come looking for them, and that no one was at the house. "They're driving an older red Chevrolet pickup with a crew cab."

Luna listened for a beat, then said, "I'm not guessing. I know that's the case, and I expect you to get a search going to find my friend." Luna provided her name and phone number and disconnected.

"That's just crazy. They act like I don't know what I'm talking about. Well, I'm standing right here looking at it with my own eyes while she's sitting in an office," Luna fumed.

"Let's all call in and give 'em the same info. Maybe that'll light a fire under 'em," Zee said.

"Was it Geraldine again?" Fitz asked.

"No. This was some other woman."

"Let me try Geraldine and see if we get any more support."

Fitz asked to speak to Geraldine.

"You're calling me twice in one day. This can't be good," she said.

"You're right. It's bad. Did you hear about the abandoned car they found on Glade Farm Road? It belongs to the friend whose phone you just tried to locate. I believe she went to a house where we located an abducted teen and was caught by the men who live there. I'm at the house, but no one is answering the door, and their truck is gone."

"You're telling me you think they kidnapped her and took off?"

"That's exactly what I'm telling you," Fitz replied.

"I don't guess you got a tag number off of the truck?"

"No, I failed to do that. It did have a University of Georgia tag on the front."

"Fitz, that'll eliminate maybe three trucks, you know. Can you at least give me a description of the people?"

"Sure. The men are White, in their early twenties, and appear to be brothers. They have black hair, blue eyes, and bushy beards. Katía is Black, in her fifties, and fit. The teen we saw was brunette. Your office has a picture of her. I don't know what the other teen looks like."

"OK, Fitz. Let me get this straight. If you're right, then we're looking for an older model red Chevrolet pickup with three young White men with black hair and bushy beards, two White teens, and one-middle aged Black woman."

"Correct," Fitz replied.

"OK. Let me see if we can get an APB put out. It sounds like this woman is important to you."

Fitz was as surprised by her statement as he was by his answer. "She is."

CHAPTER 20

Fitz cast his eyes to the ground, where he noticed a beetle battling through the grass. *I wonder if it knows where it's going. Does it follow some scent on the air, or does it just crawl randomly till it finds what it's looking for? I need a scent, a clue, something that will help me find Katía. Random hunting will make me too late.*

Ben was talking. His words hadn't registered at first, but then Fitz noticed he was giving his address.

"Just drop it off at the curb in front of the house. … No, I'll pay for it. Here's the credit card number."

"Ben's having Katía's car towed to his house," Luna explained as she walked up to Fitz. "Do you have any idea how we can find her?"

Fitz tugged his beard and looked out to the lake.

"You're gonna pull out all the hair if you keep doin' that," Zee observed.

Luna's question pressed on Fitz's heart. "I can't think of anything to do other than wait to see if they get a hit on the

APB. Until then, I have no idea where to even begin." He reached into his little pouch, but there were no more M&Ms.

"We could just ride around. If Lady Luck smiles on us, we might run across 'em," Zee said. "If we split up into one car per person, it would multiply our chances."

Fitz put his hand on Zee's shoulder. "Unfortunately, that's probably our best chance. The odds of us finding the truck that way are nearly zero, though."

"I have to do something," Luna protested. "I can't stand going home knowing Katía and those girls are in the hands of three maniacs."

"If I was one of them brothers, where would I go?" Zee mused.

"I suppose they could own property elsewhere. We should be able to find out with some research." Ben added.

"How long would that take?" Luna asked.

"I don't know," Ben admitted.

"If they're running from the law, I don't think they'd go to one of their properties," Fitz said. "They'd look for somewhere else to hide, somewhere no one knows about."

"Like an abandoned building or vacant house," Ben mused.

"We need to get inside their heads and think like they'd be thinking," Fitz said. "Why would they leave after hiding here so long? What was different?"

"Probably Katía showing up," Luna answered. "They were afraid we or the police would come looking for her."

Fitz looked back at the beetle, which had progressed about a foot. *So she was still alive when they left.* The beetle pulled up and over and around blades of grass, each blade seeming a major hurdle to one so small.

Fitz identified with the beetle, feeling small and in the midst of a massive struggle. But there was something more there, beyond the daunting nature of the task at hand. There was an ache. *I haven't felt anything like this since Sharon.*

He redoubled his effort to identify where the men might have gone. *I have to find her. Where would they go? Out of state?* Ben was talking.

"I bet they already knew about wherever they went. They don't seem like the types to delve into researching a location."

It dawned on Fitz just how little he knew about the three brothers. "We don't even know their names. Did they buy this place, or was it their parents' home? How long have they lived here? We need to know more about them."

Zee eyed the house. "We might find some info inside."

"My lock-picking tools are back at the park," Fitz said, cursing himself for not having brought them.

Ben hurried toward the front of the house. "Maybe they left a key for us."

The others followed, and Fitz smiled when Ben pulled a key from under the doormat.

"I believe they just invited us in," Ben said. He unlocked the door, and the park pals filed inside. "Look for a desk or file cabinet."

They spread out, moving through the various rooms till Luna called, "Got it!"

She had found a kitchen drawer stuffed with bills and other documents. "The power bill is addressed to Earnest Inmanson." She continued digging through the drawer, setting papers on the table.

While they were searching through the papers, Fitz wandered from bedroom to bedroom. The first one he entered was an odd L-shape. Expecting to find a mirror image in the next bedroom, he was surprised when it was rectangular.

"I just figured out why the deputies didn't find Sadie," he called out.

Ben and Zee came into the bedroom while Luna kept combing through the documents.

"What are you talking about?" Ben asked.

"Come look at this," Fitz said and led the way back to the L-shaped bedroom. "Look at that. They've built a room with no doors."

"There's gotta be a hidden door somewhere." Zee stated.

"My guess is they got to it through the attic. This old house has a nice, high space up there," Fitz observed.

"Wow! I'm gonna check it out," Zee said. Finding the pull-down stairs in the hallway, he climbed up. "It's plenty warm up here. … Yep. There it is. There's a hole and a ladder leadin' down. They've got three cots set up. I reckon they're plannin' on kidnappin' three girls."

"One for each guy," Luna said, startling Fitz, who had not heard her walk up behind him.

"That's creepy," Ben added.

The sound of crunching gravel drew Fitz's attention.

"It sounds like we have company," Ben said, moving to look out the front window.

"I think I'll come down," Zee stated. "Down with the bad. Down with the bad," he repeated to remember to lead with his sore knee. "I sure wouldn't want to be up there in the heat of the day."

"Great. It's a deputy." Ben announced. "I think it's too late to run out on the porch and act like we just got here."

"Maybe he'll forget about us breakin' in when we tell him about the invisible room," Zee said, rubbing his hands together.

"I hope you're right. Here he comes," Luna observed.

"You know him?" Ben whispered as the deputy, a tall, strapping Black man of about thirty-five years, neared the porch.

"Nope," Fitz answered.

Fitz stepped through the door, which they had left open, and said, "Good morning, Deputy."

The deputy stopped in his tracks, a cloud of confusion forming on his face. "Good morning. Do you live here?"

Fitz replied, "No. I suspect we're here about the same thing you are. A friend of ours has disappeared, and we suspect she was kidnapped by the men that live here."

"Yep, that's why I'm here. Now kindly explain why you are in the house and where the men that live here are."

"We knocked, but no one answered. They kindly left a key under the mat, so we let ourselves in to see if we could find any clues as to what had happened."

Zee stepped out onto the porch behind Fitz. "You gotta see this, Deputy." He waved for the deputy to come in, and he followed. Holding out his hand to Fitz, he said, "Deputy Lawson Anderson."

"Fitz Fitzgerald," Fitz replied, shaking his hand.

Deputy Anderson eyed him, and Fitz knew what he was thinking. Without a word, he followed Zee into the house.

"They built a room with no doors or windows to hold their captives in," Zee said. "The only way in or out is through the attic. Come on." Zee started to step up with his left foot, but the pain prompted him to switch to the right. "Up with the good. If ya got a flashlight, it would help."

When Zee stepped into the attic and Deputy Anderson was halfway up, Luna said, "I'm going, too."

They all gathered around the hole in the ceiling. "Please tell me none of you have been down there," Deputy Anderson said. "This looks like a crime scene. Everybody out."

The park pals filed down the ladder and gathered in the living room. When Deputy Anderson stepped off the ladder, he said, "I mean everybody out of the house. I realize you have a missing friend and Mr. Fitzgerald is famous in law enforcement circles, but we have to handle this correctly or we might lose our case against these guys."

Seeing Luna's hands land on her hips, Fitz looped his arm through hers and tugged her toward the door before she could say anything.

"I was about to give him a piece of my mind. Why did you drag me out?"

"Because you were about to give him a piece of your mind," Fitz chuckled.

Remaining on the porch, Fitz could feel the sun beginning to heat the land. He could hear Deputy Anderson requesting the crime scene unit. While the land was heating, a chill settled in his heart. *I have to get Katia back. I hate to think what they're doing to her.*

"Now what do we do?" Luna asked.

"I wish I knew," Fitz replied.

CHAPTER 21

Fitz rattled his mind, hoping a way to rescue Katía would fall out. He realized the other park pals were waiting on him for an idea, which increased his stress level. He stuck his hand back in the pouch. *Oh, yeah. They're gone.* An idea finally surfaced, and he said, "I think we should go to Ben's house and see what we can learn about these three guys."

"The only place you folks are going is the sheriff's office," Deputy Anderson announced. "We're going to have to question all of you."

"You can't arrest me. I've done nothing wrong," Luna fumed.

"I didn't say a thing about arresting you," Deputy Anderson replied. "I have two incensed parents that showed up from Texas wanting to know why we can't find their daughter after we let them know we might have a lead. Now everybody has disappeared except for you four. Sheriff Tucker wants answers. I need you to drive to the sheriff's office right now." He stood straight and tall, his demeanor leaving no room for questions.

"I guess that answers my question about what we're doing next," Luna huffed and started toward the 4Runner.

Fitz started to step off the porch, then turned and asked, "Which office do you want us to go to?"

"The main one on Brown's Bridge. Sheriff Tucker will be waiting."

After stopping by Laurel Park to pick up their cars, the park pals regrouped in the parking lot of the building in which the sheriff's office was located. Fitz restocked his pouch with M&Ms.

"Why you think they made us come down here? They know everythin' we do already," Zee said.

"Are you worried they're going to nab you?" Ben chuckled.

"Naw. I'm clean as a whistle."

"I wonder what that phrase even means," Ben replied.

"I got no idea, but it fits me to a tee."

"There's another odd phrase. You're just full of them today," Ben said as they reached the door leading into the building.

Fitz led the way to the sheriff's office and held the door while the others entered.

A familiar voice sounded from the desk. "Well, I never thought I'd see the day when Fitz Fitzgerald walked through those doors again."

"Hey, Geraldine," Fitz replied.

"You must be in big trouble this time. Get called to the principal's office?" Geraldine, a dark, heavy-set woman with a winsome smile chided.

"No, I'm not in trouble."

"Well, come on in and make yourself at home. I hear Sheriff Tucker himself wants to question you."

Sitting down, Fitz tried to relax his shoulders, which had risen nearly to his ears. He found himself tugging at his beard and tried to stop that, too. He couldn't stop himself from going for the M&Ms.

"Are we just supposed to sit here and wait while Katía and those girls are in danger?" It was Luna. "We need to get busy finding them."

"Ma'am," Geraldine began, "Talking with Sheriff Tucker is the best thing you can do to help them. Your information could be what leads our deputies to them."

Ben patted her on the shoulder. "It's OK. We need time to think about how to find them, anyway." He leaned his head against the wall behind the chair and closed his eyes.

Fitz couldn't sit still, so he got up to pace. He had made one lap when Sheriff Tucker hurried into the room. "Come with me, please." He led them into a small conference room and closed the door.

"If it's not my favorite group of crime solvers and troublemakers. How are you doing, Fitz?" He held out his hand.

"Worried."

"We're going to try to help with that." The sheriff shook hands with the rest of the park pals and gestured for them to sit.

"It appears you have stumbled onto some serious crimes, so we're just going to ignore issues like trespassing and breaking and entering."

"We didn't break anything," Luna argued.

"Anyway," Sheriff Tucker continued, "I have two very concerned parents and three guys who allegedly have disappeared with their abducted daughter."

"They have another girl and our friend, Katía, too," Luna added.

"Right." Sheriff Tucker rubbed his hand over his jaw.

Fitz realized the sheriff was really concerned. "How can we help?"

"I need to know everything you know."

"We think there are three brothers living in the house. They appear to be in their early twenties, all with black hair, blue eyes, and bushy beards. We showed Deputy Anderson the room they had constructed to keep the girls in. Though we didn't actually see a second girl, we're assuming they also have the one abducted at a bus stop in Toccoa since the perpetrators' descriptions match these young men. I also suspect they were behind the failed attempt to abduct a girl in Denver, South Carolina."

"I know you reported the note in the bottle found on the lake, but how did you folks locate these guys?"

Luna explained. "We studied the map for possible tracts of land that could be farms, then knocked on the doors and told them we were looking for Sadie. We wanted to see how they responded. We followed up at the places that seemed suspicious. Finally, Katía got the photo that showed Sadie was in the three guys' house."

"You probably don't want to know any more about our search," Fitz added.

Sheriff Tucker eyed him, appeared to agree, then asked, "Did you come to any conclusion as to what they plan to do with the girls?"

"I have no idea, but it cain't be good," Zee said. "They built a cage in the house to hold these girls. That ain't right in the head."

"Why do you think your friend was abducted, too?"

"Her car was abandoned near the house. She has a caring heart and probably went back by herself to get more proof so you could get another search warrant but then got caught. That's my guess," Ben said. The others nodded.

"Now for the million-dollar question. Where do you think they went?"

Fitz tugged his beard. "I suspect they went somewhere they are familiar with. It would need to be isolated, abandoned, and provide shelter. My hunch is they're not the camping type, but I guess they could have taken a tent and headed for the woods."

Sheriff Tucker's eyes narrowed, intensifying the stress lines on his forehead. "You realize I have to call another set of parents and tell them we think we know who has their daughter, but we have no idea where they are."

"Sorry about that," Zee said.

"I assume you've already started looking into other properties these guys might own," Fitz suggested.

"It appears that the farm on the lake is all they own. It's been in the Inmanson family for four generations. The boys inherited equal shares when their mom died three years ago. The father died five years before the mom."

"Do they have jobs?" Fitz asked.

"We haven't found any record of employment yet. They might be living off insurance money."

"Strange," Luna mused. "What would set them off so they decided to start abducting girls?"

"It's usually some sort of abuse or trauma from childhood," Sheriff Tucker replied. "Do you have anything else you need to tell me?"

The park pals looked at each other. Fitz finally said, "Not that I can think of."

"OK, then. Thanks for coming in. I expect you to leave this alone and let my deputies handle it from here on," Sheriff Tucker said, looking each one in the eye. Holding out his hand to Fitz, he added, "You staying sober these days?

We could use you back on the force. At least we could keep an eye on you that way," he chuckled, the stress lines relaxing for a brief second.

Sheriff Tucker escorted them back to the waiting room. "Take care of yourselves. And please stay out of this investigation."

"Thank you for your hard work," Fitz said, and the group exited the office.

On the way to the car, Ben said, "You don't think he was serious about us staying out of this, do you?"

CHAPTER 22

The park pals gathered at Ben's house. Fitz paced the den. *How could she have been so stupid! She should have called. I'd have gone with her. What can I do? I have to find her!*

"I trust your mind's workin' as hard as your feet," Zee said to Fitz as he passed by.

Fitz didn't respond. He had flashed back to the day he got the call about Sharon's death. He had paced the camp that day, lost in a sea of humanity. Searching till he found an empty tent, he went in. Darkness enveloped him from without and within.

"Hey, Fitz. Are you OK?"

It was Ben's voice breaking through the darkness. Disoriented, Fitz discovered he was in a storage closet in the dark. He found the doorknob and turned. The door swung open and light flooded in.

Embarrassed, Fitz said, "Sorry. Flashback," and walked out to join the others. *I'm not asking how long I was in there.* "What ideas have we come up with?"

"So far, I think you were right to start with," Ben replied. "It's either going to take a stroke of luck or a hit on the APB. Unfortunately, I don't think they'll let us know if they get a hit on the APB." He sat at the computer and locked his eyes on it.

"What are you studying so hard?" Fitz asked.

"I'm looking for that stroke of luck on traffic camera feeds."

Zee sat at the counter with a bagel, and Luna sat next to him, studying her phone.

"I'm guessing they headed toward Lula or Cleveland, so I'm watching the feed from the camera at Lula Highway and Three sixty-five," Ben added.

Fitz tried to rein in the angst and get his mind in gear. He kept having to push away images of what they might be doing to Katía. He looked at the M&Ms he had just pulled out of the pouch. *These aren't helping.*

He had just banished an image of her strapped to a chair being tortured when Ben said, "I think that's them."

The others surged to look over Ben's shoulder as he stopped the feed and zoomed in on the truck. "That's definitely a bushy beard," Zee said.

Fitz cringed when he saw Katía hog-tied in the bed of the truck. "Where's the next camera?"

"I don't think there is another one in Hall County," Ben replied.

"You mean that's it? That's as far as we can track her?" Fitz groaned.

"We should let the sheriff's office know," Luna said.

"We can't do that without telling them how we found out," Fitz replied.

"I could call in an anonymous tip," Luna added.

"With caller ID, there's no such thing anymore, unless you can find a pay phone," Ben pointed out.

"What if I call the Habersham sheriff's office?"

"That sounds promising," Ben said.

"Can you get the tag number?" Fitz asked.

Ben worked with the computer and squinted his eyes. "I can't tell if it's covered up or has been taken off."

"There's not much point in calling Habersham, then. Besides, they could be out of the state by now," Fitz said.

"But they could just as well still be in Habersham County," Luna said as she pressed dial. She explained the situation to the deputy who answered. "I'd prefer to remain anonymous," she said when he asked for her name. "I don't know the tag number, and I believe they may have removed it or covered it up. … Just trust me. The lives of two teenaged girls and a woman are in your hands." She disconnected the call.

"Well done," Ben said.

"I don't think they went out of state," Fitz said.

"What makes you think that?" Ben asked.

"They seem like simple folks that don't leave the farm much. I'm betting they went somewhere associated with their past … some place they already knew would be vacant."

Ben rubbed his hand through his hair. "That still leaves us with a huge area. There's no way we can figure out where they've gone."

"Not without knowing more about them," Fitz said, a flicker of hope sparking. "Search the newspaper archives for everything you can find on these Inmansons."

"That's a tall order. It'll take a while," Ben replied.

"Inmanson isn't a common name, so there shouldn't be that much to sift through," Luna pointed out.

Ben pulled up the newspaper site and said, "You're right. Maybe it won't be that daunting."

"I just had a random thought," Luna said. "I bet their house was there before the dam was built. It used to be riverfront property."

"Yeah, the house looks old enough," Zee added. "They don't build 'em like that anymore."

"Well, look here. The three boys are in a picture from Vacation Bible School at Clemons Chapel," Ben said. He kept searching.

Fitz stood still, looking out the kitchen window. "I wish Snickers hadn't found that bottle."

"No, you don't," Luna replied. "If she hadn't, no one would know where Sadie was."

"We still don't know where she is, and now Katía is in their hands, too," Fitz answered.

"We're closer to finding them than we were before," Ben said. "I've found obituaries for folks I assume are the guys' mom and dad. Here's a photo of the boys at a church camp. They must have been quite the religious family."

"Or the parents wanted them out of the house for a while," Zee chuckled.

"Which camp did they go to?" Fitz asked.

"It says Tugaloo Trails."

"See what you can find out about it," Fitz added.

Ben worked the mouse and tapped on the keyboard. "It says it was in Stephens County and closed in 2009. It's on the river at the southern end of Yonah Lake. It was a Baptist camp. These are ecumenical folks."

"Who's operating it now?" Fitz asked. He watched as Ben's eyebrows scrunched together while he studied the screen.

Finally Ben said, "I don't see anything about its being in use now. I guess it's still closed."

"Closed as in abandoned?" Fitz asked.

"I would assume the church still owns the property. Let me pull up the satellite view."

The group converged around Ben and the computer again.

"Looks like a pretty spot," Zee said.

"Yeah, but it's not being kept up. You can see areas around the buildings have grown up with trees and weeds. I would expect there to be grass there," Ben observed.

"There's nothing close to it. Just woods," Luna said.

"The site said the camp property covered two hundred acres," Ben added. "It is in the right direction for where they were headed. Are you thinking what I'm thinking?"

"That it would be the perfect place to hide out?" Fitz asked. "And it's a place they know about from their childhood. There's a good chance they've taken Katía and the girls there. Let's go."

"Wait a minute, Fitz. The sheriff told us to stay out of this. I think we should call and tell him our suspicions," Luna said.

Fitz halted on his way to the door and squelched a sudden surge of anger. "You can call him if you like, but I'm going out there. I don't think they'll enter private property on a hunch."

"Let me get my gun, and I'll drive," Ben said.

"I'll call the sheriff on the way," Luna added.

CHAPTER 23

There was no way to get comfortable. A bump in the road punctuated that truth, sending a surge of pain as the hard truck bed transferred upward energy into Katía's head. Hogtied with duct tape and her mouth taped shut, she lay on her side with the steel digging into her hip and shoulder.

Fear intensified each pain as the truck zoomed along. She had tried to get onto her knees, but couldn't keep her balance, earning what she was sure would become a large bruise on her chin.

Earnie's words kept roiling in her mind. When Everett had asked what they were going to do with her, he had said, "Remember the cave where we used to hide?" She was sure that's where they planned to dump her body. *Lord, they put your body in a cave. Francis of Assisi would have been grateful to have the chance to end up like you. Please help me not to fear and let me trust you to walk with me through this valley of the shadow of death.*

That she had not pled for her life surprised her. *There are worse things than death, much worse. Just think what these girls are going to have to live through. Think of the torture their parents are feeling. Lord, please give me a chance to help them. I don't know how, but you can work out a way.*

The last thought brought a wave of peace. Instead of wondering what would become of her, Katía searched for ways she might get Sadie and Laurie rescued. *Surely they'll cut my legs loose to get me to that cave. It would be easier than carrying me. That will be my best chance. Ah! Maybe I could grab one of their phones and dial 911. … Unless they were smart enough to turn them off. Or have a screen lock. Wait, can't you make an emergency call even with the screen locked?*

Thinking through possibilities served to pass the time till the truck slowed and turned onto a rough road. Ruts and rocks served to pummel Katía as a canopy of trees blocked the burning sun. The bouncing truck bed forced her to shift her attention to trying to keep her body from being battered. She braced with her knees, hands, and feet as best she could, but her upper body was at the mercy of the random pounding.

The truck stopped, and Katía tensed even more than when she had been battling the bumps. She lifted her head but could see only trees.

The door opened, and she heard Everett say, "This don't look as nice as I remember. Come on out, Laurie. I'm sorry we had to brang ya out here, but we gotta hide out fer a while."

"Yeah, I thank this place has gone to pot. I just hope they's a cabin with a roof that don't leak." That was Earl. "We gonna tend to the one in the back first?"

"She ain't goin' nowhere. Let's look around."

Katía was sure it was Earnie who spoke last. Being the oldest, he was their leader. She still puzzled over the way they treated Sadie and Laurie. *Why are they being so nice to people they've kidnapped?* The voices trailed away till she could no longer make out what they were saying.

I can't move fast, but if I can get out of this truck, I can inch away. Maybe they'll be gone long enough for me to hide. She squirmed and wiggled her way to the back of the truck, then tried to get up on her knees. *Nope.*

She pivoted onto her back, worked her feet over the tailgate, and tried to pull up with her hands. After five attempts, she realized it wasn't going to work. *The only way out of here is to open the tailgate.* She wiggled to the center to see if she could get her hands to the latch.

"She's tryin' to get away!" Earl's voice pierced both the silence and her heart.

"Let's watch. I wonna see this," Earnie laughed.

With her spirit deflating, Katía slumped.

Earl laughed and slapped his thigh. "I ain't never seen such a sight. Look how she's a layin'. Hey, Earnie. How we gonna get 'er to that cave? I ain't carryin' 'er."

"We could make Everett carry 'er," Earnie snickered.

"I ain't carryin' 'er that far," Everett countered.

"We need to go ahead and get rid of 'er," Earnie said. "I reckon we'll have to cut 'er legs loose. Get another rope to make sure she cain't run away."

Katía searched within and was surprised she wasn't panicking. Instead, she found a peace that only the Holy Spirit could have provided. She closed her eyes and prayed aloud, "Dear loving God, thank you for being with me. Amen."

"She's prayin' again," Everett whispered. "It ain't right to kill a prayin' woman."

"Shut up, Everett," Earnie said.

"What if she's prayin' when you shoot 'er? God'll get us fo' sure. You know what Mama used to say."

"Quit worryin' about it," Earl scolded. "She's gotta go, or she'll spoil the whole plan."

They walked toward the truck, Earl and Everett holding the ropes tied around Sadie and Laurie like leashes. The girls' eyes were round with terror. They each met Katía's eyes, then quickly looked away.

"Can't you see you're terrifying these two girls?" Katía said. "They don't want any part of your evil plans."

"Shut up. Ain't none of your business," Earnie replied.

Sadie stopped, causing Earl's arm to jerk back. "You can't kill her. That's just evil, and she's right. I don't want any part of your plans."

"You won't have to watch," Earnie said. He tied the rope tightly around Katía's waist, then pulled a hunting knife from its sheath and added, "Be still or I'm liable to cut you." He leaned in and sliced through the duct tape binding her hands to her feet, then the tape binding her feet together. With a jerk on the rope that nearly pulled her from the tailgate, he said, "Get down."

Katía complied, climbing off the tailgate and hopping to the ground. She watched as Earl pulled the shotgun from the truck, then tried to hand Katía's pistol to Everett.

"I ain't takin' that. I don't want no part of killin' a prayin' woman. God'll send my soul to Hell."

Earnie fumed, "Everett, you wuss, bring it to me."

Everett stuffed his hands in his pockets, and Earl walked the handgun over to Earnie.

"Come on. We got a nice cave just a waitin' for you," Earnie ordered.

"Why would I walk to my death?" Katía asked.

"Because I said so." Earnie started walking and jerked the rope, nearly pulling Katía off her feet.

He's stronger than I expected. Lord, please help me figure out a way to save these girls. They don't deserve this. Katía followed, resisting here and there just to make Earnie mad.

He dragged her down an overgrown trail. Katía used her forearms to block limbs and briars from tearing at her face. Earl and Everett pulled Sadie and Laurie along. Whenever there was a clear section Katía used her fingernails to dig at the knot in the rope around her waist.

"Watch the branch," Everett said, holding it till Laurie was able to reach it and keep it from swinging back on her.

Maybe I can use Everett's sensitivity to get out of this. "You know, the Bible says, 'Thou shalt not kill.'"

"Shut up. I know what the Bible says, but David had to kill his enemies, and the Lord was OK with that," Earnie barked.

Earnie's comment caught Katía by surprise. "You're not David, I'm not your enemy, and I think your mother taught you better."

"She's right," Everett replied. "Mama did teach us we is supposed to be kind to folk."

"Shut up, Everett," Earnie yelled. "Mama ain't here, and if she was, she'd say this is what we have to do to carry out the plan."

"Well, I ain't shootin' 'er." Everett said.

"What is the plan? What are you going to do to us?" Sadie screamed. "I want to go home! You have no right to hold me prisoner!"

Earl mustered a soothing voice, "It'll get better. I promise."

Sadie planted her feet, causing Everett to run into her. "I'm not going any farther! Let all three of us go right this minute!"

"Don't make me have to discipline you," Earnie said. "Spare the rod, spoil the child is what Mama always said.

We're gonna raise you right. Earl, I guess you should do it, since she's your'n."

Katía watched anger build in Earl's eyes. Without a word, he backhanded Sadie across the cheek, nearly knocking her off her feet.

"Don't make me do that again. The next time'll be worse," Earl said.

The rage in Sadie's eyes was palpable. Katía said, "It's OK, Sadie. Don't do anything to get yourself harmed. Whether I live or die, the Lord is going to be with me. These men have no power over my soul."

Earnie backhanded Katía. "Quit talking like that. You're spooking Everett. I want you to die quietly."

Katía glared at him. "You might kill the body, but you can't kill my soul."

Everett whimpered, "Maybe we should just tie 'er up and let God decide what to do with 'er."

"That's just mean, Everett," Earl said. "That'll make 'er suffer for a long time."

Earnie grinned, "Actually, I thank that's just what she's earned."

CHAPTER 24

The Inmansons dragged Katía, Sadie, and Laurie along the trail in silence. Katía tried to think of something to say that might convince them at least to let the girls go. *Lord, I need an idea in a hurry.*

She studied Earnie's grasp on the rope. It was a death grip. *If I could break away, maybe Sadie and Laurie could get free during the distraction. I need to watch for him to loosen his grip. I just hope Earl doesn't get a shot off with the shotgun. It would be hard to hit me with the pistol.*

They continued walking, but the muscles in Earnie's forearm remained taut. Katía decided to work on Everett some more. "The Bible also says 'Thou shalt not steal.' You've stolen these two girls from their families. I don't think God is happy with you."

Earnie turned, and the rage in his eyes caused Katía's breath to catch. "Everett, hand me the duct tape. I've had enough of her mouth."

Earnie tore a strip from the roll and handed it back to Everett. As he came at her mouth, Katía pivoted and tried to break free. Earnie's grip didn't fail, and he hit her in the back of the head with the butt of the pistol, knocking her to the ground.

"I expect to be obeyed," Earnie growled.

"Stop it!" Sadie yelled. "You can't treat her like that!"

"You'll get the same treatment if you don't shut up," Earnie said, scowling at her.

"I'm a pastor," Katía said. "Do you think you should be doing this to a pastor, Everett?"

Earnie slammed her to the ground and popped the duct tape onto her face. Katía cut her eyes to the pistol he had laid on the ground.

"I'd love to see you try," he said, his voice cold as death. He picked up the pistol, then pulled her to her feet by the rope. "I should'a tied this around your neck."

Katía noticed Everett had remained silent. She hoped she had gotten to him. *My only hope is that he can stand up to Earnie when the time comes. Lord, give Everett the strength he needs to stop this evil. I'd love to live, if that's in your will, but please save these girls. I've had a good life, but theirs are just starting.*

Earnie stopped and scanned the terrain. "Ain't the trail s'posed to be around here somewhere?"

"I don't know," Earl replied. "Nothin' looks right. I don't know where we are."

"Let's go a little further."

After another hundred yards, Earnie stopped and scratched his head with the butt of the pistol. Katía saw the moment his grip relaxed in his confusion. She lunged backward with all her might. Crashing into Earl stopped her from falling. With the rope free, she rushed into the woods, weaving through trees to make herself a difficult target.

A stream of profanity followed her down the trail along with a pistol shot. She heard the bullet hit a tree high and to her right.

"Don't just stand there, shoot 'er!" Earnie yelled.

Katía braced herself for the impact of the shotgun blast as she heard someone crashing through the woods after her. The shotgun blast didn't come. Instead she heard, "They's getting' away!" *Way to go, girls.*

Katía kept running as hard as she could, luring away her pursuer in order to give Sadie and Laurie a better chance. *I know he's going to catch me, but I want to get him as far away as I can.*

She surged around a tree and hit a stand of thick briars that tore her skin and snagged her clothes. Pivoting away from them, she tripped on a high root and tumbled down the hill. Before she could get up, Earnie seized her hair and pulled her to her feet.

Seeing the murderous rage in his eyes brought an odd thought to Katía. *He must have been badly abused as a child.*

With a force that threatened to rip the hair from her head, Earnie pushed her up the hill toward the trail. The pain made it hard to concentrate on walking, and she tripped three times, increasing the agony.

Why she hadn't thought of it before, she couldn't say, but while her wrists were taped, her fingers were free. She yanked the duct tape from her mouth, and Earnie punched her in the ribs, knocking the breath out of her.

She fought to regain her breath as he propelled her up the hill. Finally, she was able to speak the words that had come to her with the realization of Earnie's past. "I'm sorry someone was so mean to you when you were a kid."

Bracing herself for another blow, she waited. It didn't come. Neither did Earnie relent on forcing her up the hill. Since she could not see his face, she was unable to gauge the impact of her words.

Finally, they regained the trail. Earnie forced her to her knees, and she finally saw his face. The fiery rage in his eyes had intensified as if a demon had possessed him. A chill ran down her spine.

Katía held her breath at the sound of approaching footsteps. Her heart sank when she saw Sadie and Laurie being dragged along, each with fresh red marks on their cheeks.

"We disciplined 'em," Earl said. "Everett was a wimp, so I had to hit his harder."

Katía felt Earnie's body shaking through his grip on her hair. *He's really angry.*

"I thank I broke my wrist," Everett said, showing the swelling. "I tripped."

"Find the cave." Those three words seemed to require a massive effort on Earnie's part. He held Katía fast while Earnie and Everett dragged the two girls on along the trail.

Rage oozed through Earnie's hand into Katía's soul. *I feel bad for him. Lord, please help heal the hurt that fuels his anger. He needs you.* Her prayer was interrupted by Earnie shaking her head, sending a new onslaught of pain. He felt the need to do that three more times before she heard Earl yell, "Found it."

Lifting up on her hair, Earnie propelled her along the trail without a word. She wished she could talk with him but didn't dare, feeling that would mean instant death. *I need to wait and look for another chance to save the girls. Now I'm sure I'm not going to make it through this.*

Earl pulled back branches to reveal a dark maw about waist high. A surge of fear hit, and Katía pulled back. It was a useless effort.

Earnie flung her to her hands and knees. "Go in."

Opening her mouth to protest, Katía thought better of it. She swallowed and crawled into the darkness. *No one will ever find me here.* She tried to squelch the gnawing fear. *Lord, I have to trust you'll be with me.*

She didn't realize she had stopped till Earnie growled, "Keep goin'. Welcome to the dyin' cave."

About ten feet in, the cave enlarged enough that Earnie stood and grabbed her hair. He flipped her onto her back and crashed his leg across her, pinning her arms. Tearing off another piece of duct tape, he covered her mouth.

"You gonna go ahead and kill 'er?" Earl called.

"Naw. Like Everett said, let's let God decide what to do with 'er. It'll give 'er time to repent. We got to get Everett to a hospital."

Everett called into the cave, "We ain't gonna hurt the girls. We're gonna train 'em to farm life so they can be our wives."

As Earnie started to leave, an impulse flashed in Katía's mind, and she kicked, tripping him.

He got to his feet without a word and hovered over her. The last thing she felt was the butt of the gun smashing into her head.

CHAPTER 25

en slowed as he approached an overgrown dirt road. "The app says this is it," Luna called from the back seat.

"They're not much for maintenance," Ben noted as he turned down the road.

"This place gives me the creeps," Luna said.

Ben jostled the Outback over the rough road till they came to what looked like it had been a parking lot before nature reclaimed it.

"That was a rough ride," Zee commented.

"Where's the truck?" Ben asked.

"If I were them, I'd hide it," Fitz said. "Let's have a look around.

"I don't see any signs of a vehicle driving through the weeds," Ben added.

They approached the closest building, which was the largest in sight. It had an inviting front porch, if you overlooked the fact that parts of the roof had caved in.

"I bet this was the dining hall," Luna said as Fitz pulled open the screen door, which fell off one of its hinges as it swung.

Realizing he had lost the element of surprise, he tried to open the wooden door quickly, but it was locked. One bang with his shoulder and the rotting wood gave, letting the door swing in. With a surge of adrenaline, Fitz rushed into the building, Beretta at the ready. Squinting into the darkness, he saw no one.

"Let's check those doors," Ben whispered, pointing across the room. "You two stay here," he directed to Luna and Zee.

Fitz and Ben crossed the open room of the dining hall to the two doors that possibly opened to office spaces. Fitz held up his hand, mouthed, "On three," then counted to three with his fingers. They popped open the doors at the same time and rushed in to find a disgusting horde of mold and mildew and holes above.

Luna didn't wait at the door. She crossed the room and entered the kitchen area. She could see daylight from another hole in the roof but found no one hiding.

"Let's keep going building to building," Fitz said.

They searched the nine cabins, two of which still had intact roofs. No one was there.

"It looks like we were wrong," Ben said after they cleared the last cabin.

"I still believe this is the place," Fitz countered.

"Maybe they decided it was too nasty and left," Luna suggested. "I certainly wouldn't want to stay here."

"It ain't swanky, but fellers could hide out in those two cabins that ain't ruined," Zee added.

They walked back to the car. Fitz couldn't believe they hadn't found Katía. *This has to be the place.* As they entered what used to be the parking lot, Fitz noticed something he had missed before.

"There," he pointed. The weeds had been bent over in what looked like tire tracks that continued about five feet beyond the front tires of the Outback. "Someone was here."

"I hate to say it, but this would be the perfect place to dump a body on their way out of state," Ben said.

Fitz glared at him, anger flashing in his eyes. The realization that Ben was right made it even worse. He caught himself before lashing out at Ben and turned and looked back at the camp. "Let's look for tracks," he said, his voice barely audible. He reached for M&Ms

"Katía!" shattered the silence, causing Fitz to startle so that he nearly left the ground. He did drop his M&Ms. "Katía," Luna yelled again.

Fitz scowled, her shrill yells scraping his already raw nerves.

"What?" Luna asked. "It's the quickest way to find out if she's here."

Without a word, Fitz began to circle the edge of the old parking area. The others fanned out, hoping to find a trace of Katía. The silence was broken only by footsteps in the weeds till Zee said, "I think they went this way."

Ben and Luna hurried over. Fitz finished his way around the parking area before coming to where they stood. Trampled weeds led north into a stand of teenaged trees along what could have been an old trail.

"Why would they go out of the camp?" Zee asked.

The most likely answer caused Fitz to shudder. He tried to swallow the dread and said, "Let's go."

As he pushed through the first branches of the trees, a hawk screeched overhead, startling him again. Looking up, he saw the hawk soaring high in the sky. To its left, five or six vultures circled in silent flight. *Don't let me be too late.*

Fitz pushed ahead, battling the small branches till the trail opened into woods with a mixture of pines, oaks, and poplars. The path, a shallow indentation in the leaf and pine needle covered ground, was more visible but offered less obvious signs of human passage.

Stopping to eye the forest, Fitz decided they probably followed the trail. Fitz pulled his Beretta. "Someone might be guarding her. I'm going to assume they followed this trail."

"That makes sense," Ben replied.

"It might lead to a place they went as kids … maybe a fire circle," Luna added.

Fitz led on, following the trail up a hill and over a ridge. The path then led them on a gradual descent with a ridge rising to their left. After a fifteen minute walk, Fitz said, "I'm not seeing any signs they were here."

"Me either," Ben answered. "Could they have just walked in a little ways, then changed their minds and turned around?"

"I think we missed somethin'," Zee said.

Fitz's heart seemed to turn over. A thought occurred that tensed his muscles. "We should have brought the dogs."

"I don't think King's that smart. He could smell 'er but wouldn't know how to lead us to 'er," Zee said.

"Snickers isn't trained that way, either," Ben added.

"I don't think she's here," Luna said. "They must have decided not to hole-up here and left."

Fitz clenched his jaw and his fists. "I don't like this." He couldn't get over the feeling that Katía was nearby, even though all the evidence said otherwise. "She should be here."

"What we gonna do now?" Zee asked.

"At this point, I think we have to let the police handle it. It looks like we've lost them," Ben said.

"No. That's not good enough. We have to find her before it's too late," Fitz pleaded.

CHAPTER 26

old. Dark. Silent. *The earth was a formless void, and darkness covered the face of the deep,* filtered through Katía's mind as she lay on the rocky floor of the cave. Not yet fully conscious, the thought seemed profound in a way she couldn't grasp. *That would make a good sermon.*

Something hard was pushing into her ribs. It registered as an annoyance. She tried to flick it away, but her hand wouldn't move. *"A formless void." Maybe that's me. I need shaping and filling. I'm so alone.* Sorrow seeped in, registering in her perception as she floated between this world and the next. *I don't want to be sad.*

Cold. Dark. Silent. Time had no meaning. The sore pressure on her rib returned. *That hurts. My head hurts. Why?* She tried to rub her head. Her hand wouldn't move. *What's on my face?* She reached for her mouth, but her hand never made it. *Why can't I touch my face? Am I dead and just can't feel it?*

The passing of time didn't register. After another three minutes, *Something's poking me in the ribs.* The soreness registered more forcibly, causing one eye to partially open.

It's nighttime, and I'm in bed. The pain in her ribs and head suggested that being in bed was not right. She pulled open the other eye. *I smell dirt.* The musty odor pulled on the tether, bringing her back from the other world into this one. Consciousness and memory returned. *I'm in the cave. That guy knocked me out. I'm hogtied.*

A surge of panic jolted her into full alertness. "Get me out of here! Help!" she tried to call, but it was muffled by the duct tape. Craning her neck to look toward the opening of the cave brought a wave of pain and nausea. No one was there.

They left me to die. To her surprise, the panic faded. A sense of peace was followed by the thought, *Though I walk through the valley of the shadow of death, I fear no evil, for you are with me. You are with me, I trust.*

Katía scanned her surroundings. There was just enough light to make out the walls of the cave. *I have to get off this rock that's digging into my ribs.* She rolled onto her back and snickered. *I'm glad no one's here to see this.* She did make quite a sight with her legs in the air and hands taped down at her ankles. *At least this is a little more comfortable.*

Eyeing the ceiling of the cave, she noticed jagged rocks in random formations. *I guess this isn't the type of cave to have stalactites. I wonder if everyone has random thoughts like that while they're waiting to die. How long do you think this will take, Lord?*

She waited for an answer. *You're right, I guess it's better I don't know that.* She lay on her back, listening to the silence. Occasionally, the sound of a breeze filtered in.

Lord, you're the only one I have to talk to. Well, I guess I could talk to myself. I don't really want to die, but it appears I am stuck. You could send someone to find me, but if it's my time to die, help me to stay connected to you all the way till you welcome me home. My back is getting tired of the rocks. It's time to roll over to the next side. I feel like a pig on a rotisserie. Chuckling at her last thought, she rolled onto her left side.

Lord, help me not to think about the suffering that's coming. In fact, you could go ahead and take me if you like and spare me all of that. But if you're not finished with me on this earth, help someone to find me. I'm sure my park pals are hunting, especially Fitz. He's not one to give up. I like Fitz. He's a kind-hearted soul, even though he doesn't want people to know it. Maybe he'll be my knight in shining armor.

I'd be easier to find if I got out of this cave. But then I'd be in the heat and would dehydrate quicker. That could be a blessing. Should I try to get out of here or just stay put? I wish my head would quit hurting.

Maybe I could get closer to the entrance of the cave so someone could see me, but I'd still be shielded from the sun. She wiggled around till she faced the entrance of the cave. Deciding she would try to get onto her knees, she rolled onto her back, leaned her knees to the left, then flung herself to the right. Her knee crashed onto the rocky floor and blocked the roll. *That hurt. At least I can see the light from the entrance like this. I wonder what time it is. Is there another way I could move? Aha!*

She rolled onto her side and squirmed her way around till her head pointed toward the entrance. She stretched her shoulder up, then pushed with her feet, achieving an inch's movement. *I'm an inchworm! This might take a minute, but I could eventually get there. Of course, there might not be any skin left from dragging over these rocks.*

I'm getting thirsty. And hungry. Lord, help me not to think about that. I have to keep my mind on you and your wonderful love. Please stay with me.

CHAPTER 27

Fitz's fists remained clenched. While he continued scanning the woods along the trail at the camp searching for signs of Katía, Zee said, "I don't think we're gonna get very far on empty stomachs. Why don't we go eat lunch and plan our next move?"

"I'm not ready to leave yet," Fitz replied.

Luna took Fitz by the arm. "Come on. We've done all we can here."

Fitz glared at her, anger and resignation battling in his heart. Luna gave his arm a tug. His feet moved, but his eyes continued scanning the woods.

"Let's find a place in Toccoa to eat and plan. If it seems best, we'll come back here and look some more," Luna coaxed.

"That sounds like a good plan to me," Ben agreed.

The first restaurant they saw was Burger King. With orders in hand, they sat at a table in the corner farthest from everyone else.

"Let's try to think like criminals. Why go there, then leave?" Ben asked, unwrapping his Whopper.

"What if the tracks weren't theirs?" Zee posed. "It could've been a hunter or someone just checking on the camp."

A pang stabbed at Fitz's heart. "That would mean we have totally lost her. I refuse to believe that."

"What if they checked out the place, then came into town to get groceries?" Luna suggested.

"That makes sense," Ben replied.

"I think they would've left someone there guardin' the girls and Katía," Zee said. "It'd be a big risk takin' 'em all into town."

The pain dug a little deeper. "Zee's right," Fitz said.

"Unless we're not dealing with the sharpest tools in the shed," Ben said.

"I think Zee's right. Even idiots wouldn't go into town with a woman hogtied in the bed of their truck," Luna replied.

"They could have left her hidden somewhere in the camp," Ben added.

"We searched the camp, remember," Zee reminded Ben.

"I still think the most logical thing is that they decided the camp wasn't fit to stay in and left. They probably drove out of state," Luna said.

Fitz pulled out his phone and dialed the sheriff's office. "Geraldine, please. ... Hey Geraldine, it's Fitz. ... No, I'm not in trouble. I just wanted to find out if there has been a hit on the APB for the red pickup. … I see. Thanks." He disconnected and rested his forehead in his hands, elbows propped on the table.

"I'll take that as a no," Ben said. "So they haven't found the truck yet. I hate to say this, but I think we might as well go home. We have no idea where to look next."

Fitz glared at him.

"Look, Fitz, I would gladly look all day and night for her if I had somewhere to look, but it appears we've lost them."

The four finished eating in silence, Fitz's gloom draining the hope out of them.

*　*　*　*　*

Before leaving the camp to take Everett to the hospital, Earnie insisted that Sadie and Laurie use the bathroom in one of the cabins that still had an intact roof. Sadie went in, came right back out, and said, "It's too nasty and there's not any water."

"Would you rather use the woods?" Earnie asked.

"I'll just go at the hospital."

"Do you think I'm stupid? You ain't goin' in the hospital."

"Fine. I don't need to go," Sadie said, crossing her arms in a huff.

"You'd better not pee in the truck," Earnie snarled. "How about you, Laurie?"

Laurie cowered behind Sadie and shook her head.

"Fine. Let's go."

After loading the girls into the truck, Earnie produced the duct tape and reached to tape Sadie's ankles together. She kicked at him. "Leave me alone!"

He wound his arm around her legs and rolled the tape around so tightly it hurt. "You're gonna learn to behave one way or the other."

He threw the roll over the truck, and Earl did the same to Laurie. "We cain't have you'uns runnin' away."

Earl sat in the back with Laurie and Sadie, holding Katía's pistol. Everett cradled his wrist and groaned as the truck bumped over the rough road leaving the camp.

Parked at the ER, Earnie said, "I'm leavin' the keys in case it gets too hot." He and Everett headed inside.

Earl shook the gun at the two girls. "Don't get no ideas 'bout hollerin' out."

"You wouldn't shoot me," Sadie challenged.

"That's a mighty big gamble to take. If you lose, you die."

Sadie stared into his eyes, trying to read him. She decided there was enough evil looking back at her that she had better not yell for help. *But if a security guard comes close, I'll try. There's no way I'm marrying one of these guys.* She scanned the parking lot for an opportunity.

When she looked to the left, the side on which Earl was sitting, she noticed him staring at her.

"You sho' are purdy," he said.

His comment infuriated her. "Shut up." Then her eyes widened when she saw a security guard making rounds on a golf cart.

Apparently, Earl noticed her interest, turned, and saw the guard, too. "I see what you's thankin'. We gotta go." He got into the driver's seat, cranked the truck, and pulled out of the parking place, driving away from the golf cart. "We'll just take a little tour till your buddy is gone."

As he drove away, Sadie's heart sank while her nerves stayed on high alert. This was the best chance of escaping she had had since they grabbed her in Texas. Had her feet not been taped together, she would have jumped out of the truck.

It was at that moment she noticed Laurie had pulled her feet into the seat and was slowly removing the tape from her ankles. Fighting to keep the surprise out of her expression, she searched her mind for a way to keep Earl from noticing what Laurie was doing.

Wanting to keep his attention on her, Sadie said, "What are you going to do to me? Why won't you let me go?"

"We done told you the plan. The sooner you accept it, the better… for all of us."

"So you really plan on me marrying you?"

"That's right. Once you learn farm life and your place as a wife, we'll get married."

"I've never done any farm work. I wouldn't know where to start." She kept battling the temptation to check on Laurie's progress. The soft ripping of tape blended with the engine noise.

"I don't like to sweat," Sadie said.

"You'll learn to appreciate it. Pickin' veggies in the hot mornin' sun'll be satisfyin'. It ties ya to the earth and your source of life. The cannin'll be worse, at least I think it is. It's so tedious it taxes my nerves. I don't like nothin' to tax my nerves."

Sadie stiffened when he looked back at her in the mirror, sensing that his angry eyes portended a message for her. Then he glanced at Laurie, and she held her breath. She didn't dare look over.

"This'uns meant for Everett. He's too gentle a soul and may need help breakin' 'er." A menacing smile followed.

Thinking it would be unnatural to not look at Laurie, Sadie turned her head to the right. Laurie glared at Earl's reflection in the mirror, hands perfectly still. Relief flooded Sadie's nerves. *I need to draw him back to me.*

"When can I go back and see my family? I miss them," she said.

"I reckon after we is married, and I don't have to worry 'bout you runnin' off."

"That sounds like too long a time. I'm ready to go now."

In her peripheral vision, Sadie noticed Laurie's feet return to the floor. "I want to go home, too," Laurie said.

"Ain't gonna happen," Earl answered, his tone reeking of finality.

"Prisoners don't make good wives," Sadie suggested.

"Shut up." Earl pulled out of the parking lot and drove down the road a way. "At least we get to run the AC this way."

He pulled into a convenience store, pulled through, then stopped at the other entrance, preparing to turn back toward the hospital. Sadie's nerves zinged, and she wanted to tell Laurie this was her chance. She looked over when she heard the door pull and Laurie's shoulder hitting the door.

"Goin' somewhere?" Earl said with the same menacing grin he had had earlier. "I love child locks."

Back at the hospital, Earl parked in the same space they were in earlier. The silence was heavy as Sadie fretted over what the repercussions of Laurie's escape attempt might be. *I'm sure we'll be "disciplined."*

After what seemed an eternity, Earnie and Everett came back out, Everett sporting a bright blue cast. Earl hopped out, holding the pistol close to his chest.

"That'un tried to get away," Earl said, jutting his chin toward Laurie. "This'un was gonna holler at a security guard. I reckon they both gonna need disciplinin'."

"True," Earnie said with a glare directed to each girl.

Earl added. "Laurie took the tape off 'er ankles."

Earnie shook his head, reached in and grabbed the tape, then said, "Stay here and keep an eye on this'un. I'll reapply the tape. I'm tempted to hogtie 'er like that other'un, but we gotta go get a 'scription filled for Everett's pain medicine." Checking that no one was nearby, he opened the door and grabbed Laurie's lower legs in a death hold. "Don't make a sound."

With the tape reapplied, they filled the prescription and drove back to camp, arriving at 2:53 p.m..

Everett asked, "Should we go check on the other'un?"

"What fer?" Earnie replied.

"To see if she's still alive. To bury 'er if she ain't."

"I consider her already buried."

CHAPTER 28

Everett twittered around the small cabin, pacing and muttering to himself. "It ain't right to just let that woman die. Mama wouldn't like it. Mama ain't happy. We cain't just let 'er suffer."

"Shut up and sit down," Earl barked. "There ain't no way 'round it. She was gonna turn us in to the police. Is that what ya want? Ya wanna go to prison?"

Everett shook his head and sat down on one of the six bunk beds.

"Now, ya reckon ya can hold onto these two? I'm gonna look for a shovel. We need a latrine, or it's gonna get real stinky in here." He started to hand Everett the rope around Sadie, then thought differently. "You only got one hand. I think I'd better tie this'un up. She's feisty." He tied the rope to one of the bed frames, pulling the knots tight. "If she tries to untie it, knock 'er out," he said, handing Everett Katía's gun. "If that don't work, shoot 'er."

Sadie caught the fleeting expression of fear that Everett flashed and sensed an opportunity. She risked a glance at

Laurie, whose eyes registered understanding. Sitting down on the bed to which she was tied, Sadie thought. *I need to give Earl time to get far enough away. Then what? I could grab Everett while Laurie makes a run for it. Would he really kill us? Maybe he'll lay the gun down. I can't wait too long, though.*

As if a gift from heaven, Sadie remembered the effect Katía's praying had on Everett. She wasn't the religious sort, but slid onto her knees, folded her hands as she had seen people do, and prayed. "Lord, Everett's in an awful mess. He's murdering Katía and standing here holding a gun, ready to kill me." She heard Everett pacing behind her.

"I don't think he's an evil person, but his brothers have led him to this low point."

"Shut up," Everett said in a low growl.

"Here I am praying for his soul, and he's telling me to stop. Have mercy on him and help him to see the light."

Everett's shove knocked her over, ramming her shoulder into the wall. "Don't you understand? It's gotta be this way. We need wives if we's gonna keep the farm goin'! That woman cain't be dead yet. I'm certain Earnie's just teachin' 'er a lesson. He'll let 'er go, you'll see." He ran his hands through his hair, eyes wild.

Sadie looked up at him and tried to generate a kind expression without letting on to her surprise that he had dropped Laurie's rope. "Everett, you know he's not going to let her go. Just think what your mama would say about all of this." Laurie was easing toward the door. "Look at me. You don't want to disappoint your mama, do you?" She held his eyes, which were wild with anxiety.

"I don't know what to do. I cain't let 'er die, but Earnie'll discipline me if I let 'er loose." His eyes pleaded for help.

I have to keep him talking and focused on me. "I'll help you make a plan, then. Maybe we could slip out tonight and let her loose. Earnie won't ever go back to check the cave. He'll never know."

"He'll know. He'll hear us leave. Why would you help me?"

Sadie swallowed hard, knowing the next lie would be difficult to speak. "If I'm going to be part of your family, don't you think I should help?" She thought she saw a tear forming in his eye.

Laurie was reaching for the door when Everett looked down at his hands. Apparently, he noticed the absence of the rope and jerked toward Laurie. She bolted out the door, running down the entrance road toward the highway. Everett looked at Sadie with a lost expression before racing after Laurie.

Sadie dug at the knots securing her to the bed frame. She couldn't budge them, so she tried the ones around her waist, breaking a nail in the process. They wouldn't give, either, and the rope was tied too tightly to slip over her head or hips. Going back to the knots around the bedframe, she was just beginning to loosen the first one when she heard the sound of an engine approaching.

She jumped up to look out the front window, only to see the red pickup rolling in with Earnie driving and Laurie and Everett in the back seat. When Laurie got out, Sadie could see a bruise blooming on her left cheek. With spirits crushed, she retightened the knot on the bedframe.

"You'd better hope the other'un is still in there," Earnie growled as he got out of the truck. "How could you let 'er get away?"

"The other'un was prayin' and talkin' 'bout what Mama would think about what we're doin', especially about killin' that'un."

"Get it through your thick head that Mama'd approve. She'd want us to keep the farm goin', and to do that we have to get rid of the one that would turn us in. Now help 'er carry the groceries while I check on the other'un."

Sadie was sitting on the bed when Earnie stormed through the door. "If you don't quit fillin' Everett's head with talk about Mama, I'm gonna put you in the cave with the other'un, and we'll start over. Got it?"

Sadie nodded even though her heart protested. *Maybe Everett will take me to save Katia tonight.*

"Where's Earl," Earnie demanded.

"Diggin' a latrine," Everett said, leading Laurie in with the groceries. "How we gonna let 'em go to the bathroom without watchin'?"

"She's gonna be your wife. I reckon you'll get to watch," Earnie replied with a sneer.

"That's gross. I won't go if Earl is watching," Sadie protested.

"Well, I guess you's gonna hold it a long time," Earnie barked back.

"Don't worry, Laurie. I won't look," Everett added.

Sadie rolled her eyes. "You realize you will be going to prison for this, and it'll be for a long time if you murder Katía."

"We're too smart to get caught," Earnie replied. "No one'll find 'er in that cave. Heck, we could just barely find it. We do have another problem though."

"What's that?" Everett asked.

"We cain't go back to the house unless you and Earl are married to these two. Then the police cain't say nothin'."

Everett scratched his head. "But sometime we gotta go check on the cows."

Sadie almost erupted and said how stupid they were and that she had no intention whatsoever of marrying any of the three. She swallowed the words when the image of standing before a judge or pastor and being able to tell them what was really going on suggested a way out of this prison. *I also know that a seventeen-year-old can't get married without parental approval. Holding my tongue will save me from being "disciplined" and won't give away our escape route. It's best to play along.* "So when are we getting married?"

* * * * *

There was light coming through the cave entrance, so Katía knew it was still daytime. She had three positions, both sides and her back, and they were all getting sore from the hard ground and rocks.

It's been a long day, Lord. My body aches. My shoulders feel like they're about to pop out of their sockets. It doesn't seem to matter whether I run them inside or outside of my knees. I'm hungry and thirsty, too. How long has it been since I've had anything to eat or drink? Help me get my mind off my body's woes.

Maybe it will help to pray for my church folks. Please remember Helen and her various aches and pains. I'm glad she was able to make it on the cruise with her family this summer. Remember Don as he goes through his radiation treatments. Please keep him strong and bring healing. Bless Sandra as she deals with her family issues. She probably needs to divorce that dirtbag husband of hers. Sorry, for that last comment, Lord.

I wonder what heaven is really like. I guess I'll be finding out soon. I look forward to actually being able to see you, Lord. That will be wonderful.

CHAPTER 29

Zee's straw slurped, then he said, "I'm gettin' a refill. Anybody else want one?"

"Thanks." Ben handed Zee his cup. "You need to eat, Fitz."

Fitz had hardly touched his meal. At Ben's prompting, he took a bite of burger.

Luna's phone alarmed, and she started reading. "It's an Amber Alert." The others' phones squawked, too. "It's about our girls! This should help!"

"Most people just ignore these, figuring they won't see the vehicle anyway," Fitz said.

"Well, I'm keeping my eyes peeled," Luna replied.

"I hate to say it, but with the police looking and everyone alerted, I don't think there's anything else we can do but go back home and wait," Ben said, finishing his last French fry.

Fitz scrambled his brain, searching for a reason to stay and keep searching. His heart ached to find Katía before it was too late. A random thought made him chuckle. *I won't ever hold back from hugging her again.* His mind lingered on the last time he hugged her.

"Care to share what's so funny?" Ben asked.

Dragged out of his thought, Fitz eyed Ben but didn't answer. Finally he asked, "If they didn't stay at the camp, where did they go?"

"Probably somewhere with runnin' water," Zee said. "In this heat, staying at the camp without water would be misery."

"A motel, maybe?" Ben suggested.

"Let's drive around and check the motels in Toccoa," Fitz said.

"Won't the police be doin' that?" Zee asked.

"Not physically. They might make some calls to ask if the guys have checked in, but if they use fake names and pay in cash, they won't get noticed," Fitz replied. "Let's go."

"I need a pit stop first," Luna said.

"I think we all do," Ben added.

While waiting for the others to finish in the bathroom, Fitz pulled up a list of motels in the area. He found four. *This won't take long.*

He directed Ben to the closest of the four motels. Ben drove around it. There was no red truck.

At the second motel, Luna pointed. "Is that it?" A red Chevrolet pickup sat near the end of the building.

"It's got a crew cab," Zee said. All four of them leaned forward as Ben drove past it.

"Nope. It's a Tennessee tag," Fitz said.

When they found nothing at the last two motels, Fitz's heart sank. He knew he should have already identified their next move, but he had nothing. Both his head and his heart were empty. He ate the last three M&Ms in the pouch.

"That was unproductive," Ben said, pulling into a parking place at the motel. "Does anyone have any other ideas? I'm all out."

"If they're smart, they'll know the police are lookin' for 'em. I'd lay low, maybe find a place in the woods to camp," Zee suggested.

"I hate to say it, but we might be barking up the wrong tree. They could be in Virginia by now," Luna said.

Her comment caused Fitz's heart to sink farther. "What are we even doing here? Luna's right, they probably fled out of state. I doubt we'll ever see Katía again."

"Now don't go sayin' stuff like that," Zee said. "If we don't find 'em, the police will. Have a little faith, man."

"Yeah, we're not totally out of options yet. When I get back to my computer, I'll see if there's a way to access the traffic cameras in Toccoa."

"It'll take us over an hour to drive back," Fitz moaned.

"I should have thought ahead and brought it with me," Ben said.

"Hind sight's twenty-twenty," Zee added.

"We need to find her in twenty-four hours," Fitz said. "Every minute counts."

"Well, let's get moving then." Ben pulled out of the parking space and headed to his house.

It was 3:55 p.m. when they got back to Ben's house. Getting out of the car, Luna said, "Not that I don't enjoy you guys' company, but I need to go get supper started. Let me know if you find anything."

"I've got a date with a certain lady that I need to get to," Zee said.

"You have a date?" Ben asked.

"Yeah," Zee said, making the shape of a wine bottle with his hands.

Ben laughed. "I see."

"But let me know if you find somethin'. I'll be ready to roll," Zee added. "Keep your spirits up, Fitz. She'll be OK. She's a fighter."

Fitz glared at Zee as his words sank in, giving a lift to his heart. "That's just what I needed to hear. She is a fighter. Let's get at it, Ben."

*　*　*　*

"I thank we should find a preacher to marry us," Everett said, holding his cast to his chest. "Mama'd like that."

"Your wrist hurtin'?" Earnie asked.

"Yeah."

"Well, take one of your pain pills. That's what they's fer."

"You're out of your mind if you think I'm marrying him," Laurie barked.

"You'll marry 'im, even if it's a shotgun weddin'," Earnie laughed.

With the two guys turned away opening Everett's pain medicine, Sadie got Laurie's attention, then mouthed, "Play along."

Laurie's eyes narrowed, then widened. Sadie hoped she understood.

Earl walked in, his shirt soaked with sweat and dirt on his pants. "We got a latrine out behind the next cabin. You OK?" he asked as Everett swallowed the pain pill.

"Hurtin' some but not too bad."

"Sorry about that. Did ya see any police while ya was out? They'll be lookin' fer us, I s'pect."

"Naw," Earnie replied.

"Did ya miss me?" Earl sneered to Sadie.

"Terribly, my liege."

Earl's face contorted with anger. "What'd she say? What's that mean?"

"Calm down, you idiot. It's what royal women used to say to their husbands," Earnie explained.

With a malicious grin, Earl said, "So does that mean you're ready for our weddin' night?"

Sadie clenched her jaw, fighting to drown the words that wanted to fly.

"We have to adjust the plan," Earnie said. "I don't think it'd be safe to return to the house till these two is married. I'll have to do mine later."

"So what we gonna do?" Earl asked.

"I guess find a preacher to do the weddin's," Earnie said.

"Don't we gotta have a license or something'," Earl asked.

"You have to go to the courthouse to get a marriage license," Sadie instructed.

"That shouldn't be hard to find. It's three-thirty. I'll run down and get 'em, then we can take these two to a preacher," Earnie said.

Sadie covered her mouth to suppress a laugh. "Um, the people getting married have to be there to get the license. You'll have to take all of us."

A flash of rage crossed Earnie's face. Sadie stiffened, expecting a backhand. He looked at Earl.

"I don't know. She makes sense though," Earl said.

Earnie surveyed Earl. "Well ya cain't go to the courthouse dressed like that."

"I didn't brang no change of clothes."

"I guess I can just pretend to be you, then," Earnie said.

"How's it gonna look if we parade these two in tied up with ropes?" Everett asked. "Somebody'll get 'spicious."

Earnie plopped down on a bed. "This is gettin' complicated."

CHAPTER 30

Katía rolled from her left side onto her back, then onto her right side. "OK, Lord, is there anything you can do to ease the pain? This position is about to pull my shoulders out of socket, and I'm hurting all over from lying on these rocks.

"Lord, help me to be grateful for the opportunity to suffer as you did while I transition from life to eternity. I know I should be hoping to see you soon, but truth be told, I'm not ready to leave this world yet. I feel like I still have things to do.

"How long can I survive without water? It seems like I read for three days. I sure don't want to lie here that long. Of course, you were in the grave three days. Lazarus was in the grave three days. I'm seeing a pattern here. If that's what you have in store for me, please help me to bear it.

"I'm sure my park pals are concerned since I didn't show up this morning. Maybe Fitz will find me. He's good at figuring things out. We've made a good team in the past. If I get through this, I'd like to spend more time with him.

"Listen to me prattling on. Lord, I trust you'll be with me. I just hope I have what it takes to keep the faith as I suffer. Lord, give me the strength and peace I need."

A calming stillness filled her heart, and she lay there smiling, forgetting about the pain as she focused on the Spirit's presence. Next, she found herself singing, "Fill My Cup, Lord," the cave adding a nice resonance to her voice.

* * * * *

Fitz sat down at the bar in Ben's kitchen but could not stay put. He was back on his feet pacing within thirty seconds.

"I'm going to have to put you outside so I can concentrate," Ben muttered.

"Sorry. I'm afraid time is running out, especially for Katía."

"Well it might help if I could focus long enough to get into these traffic cameras."

"OK, I'll go for a walk." He harnessed Buffett and said, "Come on. You need some exercise."

Fitz stepped out into the five o'clock heat. The sun was dropping in the sky, but the air still sizzled. When he got over the shock of the heat, he tried to focus his mind on planning the next step that would lead to finding Katía and the others. Buffett padded along beside him.

"I don't see why you seem to like the heat. I'd think it would feel worse to you with all that fur."

"Meow."

"I see. I guess a cat does have to have his secrets. I don't suppose you have any ideas about how to find Katía."

"Meow."

"I doubt a treat will help, but since we're right here at the car, I guess you can have some."

"Meow. Meow. Meow."

Fitz opened the door and pulled out Buffett's treat bag, then laid six treats on the sidewalk. Buffett gobbled them down, then looked up with pleading eyes.

"That's enough." Fitz refilled his pouch with M&Ms, closed the door, and resumed walking down the sidewalk. "I was sure they'd be at that camp. I must be losing my touch."

He looked down at Buffett, who didn't respond with a meow. "I'm glad to know you disagree, but then why didn't we find them?"

Buffett remained silent, walking along, tail high in the air like he owned the place.

A woman walking her Pekingese came around the corner. Buffett fuzzed up and pulled ahead on the leash.

"Give the poor dog a break," Fitz said. "We'd better cross the street so you don't attack." He pulled Buffett off the sidewalk and across the road. Buffett kept his eyes on the dog and growled all the way across. "Isn't that better than dealing with an angry woman and a vet bill?"

Buffett responded by putting his tail up and assuming an air of aristocracy.

Fitz sank back into thinking about Katía and how to find her. Anger surged in his soul. *Why haven't they found that truck? Every officer in at least five states should be on the lookout. They're going to kill Katía, I'm sure of it. What else could they do with her? I guess they could put her out somewhere, but then she knows about the abducted girls. They wouldn't leave her alive with the chance she could testify against them.*

Feeling a tug on the leash, Fitz looked down to see Buffett had stopped to scratch an itch.

"Buffett, do you have any ideas as to our next step?"

"Meow."

"Do you care to share?"

"Meow."

"I can't just take a nap and wait. It's looking like our only hope is that Ben will get into the traffic cams. If he can't find anything, I don't know what we'll do."

"Meow."

"I'm glad you're confident. I'm about to worry myself into a panic attack."

Buffett rubbed his legs, making circles around him and purred.

"Thank you. You always know how to help."

"Meow."

"You also know how to get me tangled in the leash. All right, let's get moving. It's getting toasty just standing here." Fitz wanted to turn back to see if Ben had found anything yet, but he also didn't want to interfere with his progress. He knew he was too antsy not to pace or hover, so he kept going around the block.

He was sweating by the time they got back to Ben's house. Buffett went in and sprawled himself on the tile floor in the kitchen.

"You two look hot," Ben noted.

"Yeah. It's not the best weather for a walk. Anything yet?"

"I managed to hack into their system, but I've only found three cameras. I'm scrolling through the first one now but haven't seen the truck."

Hope, which Fitz had tried to keep from ballooning, fizzled. Apparently, Ben read it on his face.

"Fitz, I've never seen you this distraught before. Are you OK?"

"I don't think one of us has ever been this close to death."

"I see. You're so worried about Katía I'm starting to think you have feelings for her."

"I have feelings for all of you. You're my friends," Fitz insisted. "Besides Buffett, you're all I have in the world."

"I'm worried, too. Let me get back to this camera."

As Ben turned his attention back to the computer, Fitz asked, "What do you want for supper? I'll get it delivered."

"How about Chinese? I'd love some sesame chicken and sizzling rice soup."

"Perfect." Fitz looked up Bluefin on his phone, asked Ben for his address, then placed the order. As he disconnected, his phone pinged. It was a text from Luna.

"Have you found anything yet?"

Fitz responded, "Ben's watching the camera footage now. So far, nothing."

"How about the APB?"

"No word on that either."

"Bummer. Keep me posted."

"Will do."

Stuffing the phone into his pocket, Fitz started pacing.

"What now?" Ben asked.

"This isn't looking good. We're closing in on twenty-four hours."

"Why are you so focused on twenty-four hours?"

"Because a high percentage of people who are abducted are found dead if they're not located within twenty-four hours."

* * * * *

Insistent pressure on her left shoulder blade dragged Katía from sleep. She had become so weary that she scooted herself to the side of the cave so she could lie on her back and prop her knees against the wall. The first thing she noticed as she awoke, aside from the ache in her shoulder blade, was her tongue. It was dry and thick.

Thank you for the nap, Lord. I wonder how long I slept. Is my tongue this way because of dehydration? I guess that's what will take me in the end. I wish I could have a chance to say goodbye to my congregation, and to the park pals, and to Fitz. I hope worrying about me doesn't send him over the edge. He's never said, but I'm pretty sure he has PTSD. Take care of him, Lord. He's going to need you.

I need you to take care of me, too. I don't know how much longer it'll be till I'm by your side. You're the only one who can get me through this. I think it's time to give up hope of being rescued and start hoping the end will hurry and come.

CHAPTER 31

Everett moved about the cabin, hands moving back and forth between the top of his head and his pockets.

"Everett, would you be still? You's makin' me nervous," Earnie said. "How am I s'posed to figure out how to get you married if I cain't concentrate?"

"Sorry. I'm just worried how we gonna sleep tonight without 'em getting' away."

"I reckon we gonna have to take shifts to keep an eye on 'em now, ain't we. Let me get back to my thankin'."

"Good idea. Maybe a preacher'd marry us without a license," Everett suggested.

"Ya gotta have a license to make it legal, idiot," Earl growled. "Ya realize if we take 'em in to get a license, they could say somethin' 'bout how we got 'em. It won't look right if their mouths are duct-taped."

Earnie stood up. "I reckon I need to go down there and check it out. I'll ask 'em if the girls have to be there to get a license."

Earl stood up, too. "It's risky goin' into town, 'specially to the courthouse. The police're probably lookin' for our truck by now. That woman has friends, and they probably figured out she's missin'."

"You got any better ideas?" Earnie barked.

"Yeah, I do. I say we put 'em in the cave with that other'un and go back to the farm. Getting' married ain't worth goin' to jail fer."

"You can't kill us. That's just cold blooded murder," Sadie shrieked.

Earl clenched his fists while Earnie stroked his beard. Earnie said, "Hadn't thought of that." He stroked his beard some more. "Might be our best option. Let's hide out here a day or two and then decide. I hate to lose two nice wives if we don't gotta."

"They ain't exactly nice, in case you ain't noticed. Especially this'un," Earl said, yanking the rope around Sadie's waist.

Earnie sat back down and ran his hands through his hair. He wasn't feeling any remorse about leaving Katía in the cave to die. She had come snooping around their house when she had no right to do so. But killing the two other girls weighed on him.

"If we promise not to say who kidnapped us, will you turn us loose?" Sadie asked.

"Like you'd really do that," Earl barked. "I don't trust 'em."

"I hate to say it, but I agree with Earl," Earnie replied. "We're in a jam and there's only two ways out. Either there's a couple of weddin's or a couple of deaths." He ran his hands through his hair again.

"We ain't killers," Everett fretted. "Mama taught us better'n that. We ain't really gonna let that other'un die, are we? Don't ya think it's time to go get 'er? I thank she's suffered enough to learn 'er lesson."

"Shut up, Everett. She's gotta go," Earl barked.

"Yeah, Everett. I've already made my peace over that'un. She either dies or we go to prison. I pick her dyin'. These two are more of a problem. They was gonna be family. I cain't figure out what to do with 'em." He tapped his forehead with all eight fingers over and over.

"I need to go for a walk and thank. Ya reckon you can keep 'em from getting' away for a while?"

"Yeah, I got 'em," Earl answered.

Earnie left the cabin and walked down the trail that led to the cave, thankful the sun had sunk low enough that there was shade on most of the trail. Running his hands through his hair, his mind and heart went to war against each other. *How did we get in this mess? If them people hadn't come snoopin' 'round, everythin' would be goin' like it was s'posed to. I've a good mind to go ahead and shoot that woman in the cave. She's gettin' what she deserves. I don't wanna have to kill those two girls, though.*

Everett's batty about what Mama might thank, but it's really Daddy who made us like this, him and his home schoolin' just so's we could help work the farm. We ain't never had the chance to get out and meet girls like normal. And now it's too late. We's strapped with the farm and don't know how to go out and meet people. If Daddy were still alive, I think I'd just shoot him, too.

His last thought caused anger to burn and sear the guilt he had been keeping buried, guilt about leaving Katía in the cave to die. He kicked at a stick lying on the trail, and it came up and hit him in the face. He cursed, picked up the stick, and threw it as hard as he could.

I have to get a grip. He sat down on a nearby rock. *I cain't focus on what could have been. I gotta focus on how we can get out of this. OK, the woman should never be found. People have been buried in worse ways. Now, what about the other two?*

* * * * *

Katía was sure the light coming from the entrance to the cave dimmed. Her body tensed. Her first thought was that someone was standing there. *Should I make noise? If it's those guys, it might be better if they think I'm already dead. But what if it's the park pals?*

She decided to chance it and screamed through the tape while wiggling around at the same time. No one came. After about a minute, she gave up. Her heart sank with the realization that it was the sun setting. Rolling over onto her right side, she looked to the cave entrance, dreading the coming darkness.

A shape registered in her mind. Among the rocks littering the cave floor was one with the distinct form of an arrowhead. *Look at that. I've never found an arrowhead before. I guess I can check that off my bucket list. A lot of good it's going to do me now.*

She resumed watching the light at the entrance and wondering how she'd feel in the dark. Her attention was drawn back to the arrowhead. *I might as well look at it. There's something about it … It has a sharp edge. It has a sharp edge! I wonder if I could use it to cut through this tape.*

Hope blossomed as the light faded. With new energy, she squirmed her way toward the arrowhead. *I have to get there before it gets dark!* It was hard, painful work. She stopped for a rest. *Lord, thank you for whoever left this arrowhead here.*

She resumed her trek toward the arrowhead. Even though it was just two feet away, it took her ten minutes to get there. She finally held the prize in her hand. *Now what? How am I going to cut the tape? Where would be the best place to start?*

She began experimenting. She couldn't bend her wrists well enough to reach the tape around them. *Wait, if I can get my legs free, I can get out of here.* Pulling her knees toward her chin, she grabbed the loop around her ankle with her left hand and sawed at the tape with her right hand. Almost immediately, she dropped the arrowhead. More squirming.

Twisting. Searching the floor. Finally, she felt its sharp edge in the midst of the other rocks.

Tightening her grip, she resumed sawing. After a couple of minutes, she checked her progress. *I'm getting nowhere. What if I saw at the edges?* She gripped tightly and attacked the edge of the tape as best she could. Something gave.

What was that? Feeling the edge of the tape, she discovered a small tear. A new wave of hope and a stretch to her cramped fingers propelled her on. *This might take a few hours, but I think I can do it! Maybe this won't be a dying cave after all.*

CHAPTER 32

Ben was checking footage from the second Toccoa traffic camera when the food delivery arrived. Fitz left his post of looking over Ben's shoulder long enough to receive the food and tip the driver. Returning to the counter, he opened the food boxes and set Ben's beside the computer.

"How about some water and a fork?" Ben asked.

"Oh, yeah. I guess that would be helpful." It took an effort, but he turned away from the computer screen to get drinks and utensils, then returned to his position behind Ben.

Ben stopped advancing the footage and said, "Here. Sit down. I'll turn the computer so we can both see." Fitz hopped onto the stool next to Ben, and they resumed scrutinizing the footage while eating their meal.

After catching up to the current time on the second camera, Ben stood and stretched. "So far, nothing. When did it start getting dark in here?"

"I don't know. I hadn't noticed till you mentioned it."

The sun was setting and taking its light with it. Ben went around and turned on a few lights. "OK. One camera to go. I don't have much hope, though."

Fitz took the last bite of his beef and broccoli, then took the container to the trashcan. "I hope we're not wasting precious time. I still have a hunch they're in Toccoa, though."

Ben walked back to his stool and looked at his half-eaten box of sesame chicken. "This needs warming." After running it through the microwave, he resumed scrolling through the third camera's footage.

Fitz perched next to Ben and studied the images intently. His stress grew with each frame that passed. By the time they finished, his teeth and fists were clenched. A bead of sweat ran down the side of his forehead. "I can't believe we didn't see the truck." More M&Ms were required.

There had been seven red pickups, but when Ben zoomed in on each driver, it wasn't one of the guys they were hunting.

"That cost us a couple of hours. Now what do we do?" Fitz asked, not realizing he was pacing.

"Unfortunately, I can't see anything else to do but wait and hope the police catch them. They have more eyes than we do," Ben said. "You're welcome to stay here tonight if you like."

"Thanks, but I need to get back to my routine," Fitz replied, feeling the need to be alone with the strong emotions running around in his heart.

"All right, just don't do anything stupid."

"Like what?"

"Like drive all over north Georgia hoping you'll find them."

"I won't. Come on, Buffett." He picked up Buffett rather than harnessing him and headed for the door. "See you in the morning."

"Have a good night."

Fitz and Buffett settled into the car, and Fitz pondered where to spend the night. "I need to pick up more coffee. Let's stay at Walmart tonight."

"Meow."

Fitz located his favorite coffee, then perused the cat treat section. *What's this?* He picked up a goodie in a squeeze bottle. *That's interesting. Let's see if Buffett likes this. I won't need a spoon.* At the head of the self-checkout lane, a Midnight MilkyWay bar caught his attention.

Back at the car, he dished up Buffett's treat. Judging by the lapping and purring, Fitz decided it was definitely a hit. *I'd better eat this chocolate bar before it gets too hot.* The rich chocolate helped soothe his nerves a bit.

"Buffett, I don't think I'm going to be able to sleep tonight. Don't be surprised if we end up at Waffle House."

"Meow." Buffett nudged Fitz's chin and purred before settling into his lap. Fitz donned his headlamp and tried to concentrate on reading his current book. He kept shaking his head and trying to find his place when he realized his mind had drifted off to Katía. Finally, he gave up and put the book down.

"I've failed her, Buffett. It's been twenty-four hours, and I haven't found her." Sadness seeped in, and his heart felt as dark as the night sky. "I hate to think what they have done to her."

To stop thinking those dark thoughts, he tried to plan out his day for tomorrow. *Hit the park. Then what? I need a plan for resuming the hunt for Katía ... or at least those girls. What can we possibly do that we haven't already tried? Maybe I'll go back to that camp and look around again. We could have missed something.*

After his thoughts ran in about fifty circles, he reclined his seat, rolled the windows up so they were cracked, and said, "I guess I might as well try to sleep." Buffett was already sleeping soundly.

Fitz went through a relaxation ritual. Starting at his feet and slowly working his way up, he relaxed his muscles. It didn't work. His mind was still antsy. *I can at least be still and let my body rest even if my mind won't.* The moon moved into view through his windshield. He thought about Sharon briefly, but his mind jumped right back to Katía. Somewhere in the night, sleep sneaked in and took him away from the worry.

Bathed in the light of the moon, Fitz dreamed of a full moon shining on a river. Sharon stood in the river pointing. He followed her finger. Katía was standing in a cave, a hand reaching toward him in desperation. He tried to get to her, but a huge fallen tree blocked the path. She kept reaching for him, eyes pleading. He stopped and looked at his surroundings. He was on the trail they had been on earlier that day. He looked back to Sharon. She nodded her head.

Fitz awoke with a start, causing Buffett to jump to the passenger seat. "I think I know where she is!"

* * * * *

Katía's fingers cramped with a vengeance, causing her to drop the arrowhead yet again. Darkness had blanketed the cave long ago. She had no idea how long she had been sawing at the tape, progressing minimally. Hope had dissipated with the loss of light. She had no idea how long ago that was. She kept at the sawing because there was nothing else to do.

No longer believing she would escape, she rolled to her side while stretching her hands. *I have to rest. What if I go to sleep and never wake up? I have to keep fighting. Right now, I just can't. Lord, I'm going to trust you to wake me up, either here or in heaven.*

The cramps subsided. She relaxed her muscles and closed her eyes. Sleep claimed her until a sound registered in her mind. Slowly, the sound pulled her from dead sleep to groggy alertness. *It's an owl.* She listened as the hooting continued. "Was that your alarm clock, Lord? Thank you."

Discovering she was on her side and her hand was empty prompted a wave of panic. "How am I going to find that arrowhead in the dark? OK, don't panic." She took a deep breath and let it out slowly. "Usually it lands directly under my hands, and when I roll onto my side, it's just behind them."

She scooted backwards a bit, then began systematically sliding her hands along the floor. On her third sweep, she felt the familiar shape and was able to retrieve it. "Thanks again, Lord. Please give me the strength to continue." Taking a deep breath and blowing out slowly, Katía rolled onto her back and resumed sawing the tape.

Ten minutes later she transferred the arrowhead to her left hand and took a break, stretching her right fingers against more cramps. *What's with all these cramps? Is it the odd angle I'm working at or dehydration? Maybe a little of both? Lord, give me strength to carry on. And if you could stop the cramps, that would be helpful, too. I know I can't do this without your intervention.*

CHAPTER 33

Fitz parked on the side of the highway near the camp's entrance road. Buffett raised his head from where he was sleeping on the passenger seat.

"I'm going to be gone for a little bit. You're in charge till I get back." Buffett laid his head back down. Fitz checked his watch. It read 3:09 a.m. He closed the door as quietly as he could, holstered the Beretta, then headed up the road. He fought the urge to hurry. He also battled doubt, wondering why he thought he could find her just because she appeared in a dream. *Am I losing my mind? Why am I even here? I felt so certain when I woke up. I'll keep going. I don't have any better leads.*

He walked carefully and quietly, focusing on care over haste. The moonlight illuminated a shape up ahead. As he got closer, he realized it was the truck. *Maybe I'm not so crazy after all.* He stopped to plan how to get around the cabins without being seen. *I could try cutting through the woods, but I might never find the trail. I'm going to skirt the parking area and hope they're asleep.*

Turning right, he followed the tree line, searching for the path that led past the cabins and to the trail they had followed yesterday. That path appeared, and he took it, eyeing the cabins as he walked past them. Everything was dark and quiet. Now that he was at the end of the row of cabins, he didn't see the trail that led into the woods. He stopped and searched amidst the moon shadows.

Thinking back to yesterday, he remembered holding a branch to keep it from slinging back and hitting Luna as they went through. He searched for a familiar-looking tree, walking back and forth in the area where he thought the path should be. Seeing a possible trail through some branches, he pulled back the limb and slipped through, being careful not to let it rebound and awaken the guys.

Between shadows, the moon illuminated what Fitz decided was definitely a trail. He moved on ahead, still being as quiet as he could. He stepped on a stick, and it cracked before he could stop the pressure of his foot. He froze, listening for pursuers, but heard nothing.

In the night, the trail didn't seem familiar at all. He stopped and wavered. *Am I on the right path? Is this even a trail?* Fitz looked up at the moon and remembered the dream. *It seemed so real. Now I just don't know. Ben would tell me I'm crazy to have even come, but I'm here now, and the truck is here, so I'm going to trust my instincts.* He pressed on.

When he felt he was far enough away from the cabins, he relaxed and quit worrying about being so quiet. A new worry presented itself. *How am I going to find that cave?* He stopped about every twenty yards and studied the terrain as far as he could see. Once he stiffened, thinking he heard a sound behind him. *What was that?* He unholstered the Beretta, slowed his breathing, and remained silent, listening. Hearing nothing else for a couple of minutes, he decided it was nothing. He reached for M&Ms and discovered he'd left the pouch in the car. He continued on.

Eventually, Fitz recognized the spot where they had turned around yesterday. Anger flashed. *If we had just kept going, we might have found her.* He pressed on, moving more quickly but continuing to stop about every twenty yards for a closer inspection.

After covering another one hundred yards, doubt crept into his soul. *What was I thinking? How am I ever going to find her? I can't believe I'm doing this just because of a dream. At least I found the others. I hope I can get the girls out safely.*

He looked to the moon, hoping it would tell him whether to keep hunting for Katía or go back for the girls. A rustle to his left caught his attention. *It's most likely a raccoon.* He decided to check it out anyway.

Pushing through the tree limbs and undergrowth, he expected to hear an animal running off, but he didn't. He stopped and listened, then heard the sound again. It was straight ahead of him. He pushed on through the vegetation, hope rising. *Maybe I'm not loony.*

He broke into a clearing, and what he saw stopped him dead in his tracks: a cave. The rustling was coming from inside. *Can this be possible?* Without a thought for his safety, he lowered himself and plunged into the cave, fully expecting to find Katía. The sound came toward him, and too late he realized it was probably a wild animal.

His head crashed into something hard, stopping his momentum, then something pounded into his shoulder. "Ouch!"

"Fitz?"

"Katía?" He reached toward the voice. It was pitch black in the cave. He connected with an arm. "I can't believe I found you. Are you OK?"

"I've been better." She staggered into Fitz. "I'm feeling dizzy."

Fitz holstered the Beretta, got ahold of her, and helped her out of the cave so they could fully stand. As soon as they were out, he grabbed her in a bear hug. "I was afraid I was going to lose you."

"Ooh! Sore!"

"Sorry." He let loose.

She leaned into him. "I was hoping you'd rescue me, but I got loose on my own just in case. Would you mind taking the tape off my wrists?"

"Well, well, well," a voice boomed from behind them. "Don't move or you'll be shotgun fodder."

Fitz eased his hand toward the Beretta. "Uh, uh. That'll be your last move. Hands up." Fitz felt the Beretta slide out of the holster. "Thanks for addin' to my gun collection. You two've been mighty generous."

Katía slid to the ground. "I can't go back into that cave."

"That's exactly what you're gonna do."

"Just man up and kill me now, Earl," she said.

"That'd be too easy for the likes of you. Besides, I don't wanna give anyone reason to come lookin' 'round if they hear a shot. On the ground, old man. I was hopin' to get to use this." He slid the duct tape off the barrel of the shotgun, taped Fitz's hands together, then taped his mouth shut. "Now get in that cave."

Fitz stood but stayed put. Earl picked up the shotgun and aimed it at Katía. "You've got five seconds."

Glaring at Earl in the moonlight, Fitz squelched the urge to charge, not wanting to risk Katía's life. He bent and walked into the cave.

Earl taped Katía's mouth and dragged her back into the torture chamber. Katía tried to resist, but she had no energy.

Positioning himself at Fitz's side, Earl said, "Feet, please." Fitz didn't move, so Earl punched him in the jaw. "That was fun. Want me to do it again?" Fitz pulled up his feet. Earl taped his ankles together, then jerked his ankles up and looped tape around the bonds of his feet and wrists.

"I just love hogtyin'. It's so dignified."

After Earl had finished taping Katía, he stood over the two captives. "The best part of this is knowin' you'll get to watch your girlfriend die first since she's had a head start on ya." Earl left the cave.

Fitz's heart broke. He wanted to tell Katía how sorry he was, how he should have been more careful. Mostly, he wanted her not to have to suffer any more. The tape over his mouth prevented him from uttering the words. He rolled onto his side. In the moonlight that filtered into the cave, he saw a tear shining on her cheek.

CHAPTER 34

Zee parked by the bathhouse at Laurel Park for his morning wash-up. "We finally beat Fitz and Buffett here, King." He got out of the car and looked toward the entrance of the park, expecting Fitz to be rolling in. "That's odd. You wait here, and I'll be right back."

When Zee exited the bathhouse, Ben was getting out of his Outback. "Mornin'," Zee said.

"Hey, Zee." Ben looked around. "Where's Fitz?"

"No idea. Overslept? He say anythin' about havin' to be somewhere today? Luna said she and Carlos were meetin' with their lawyer about a will, so she won't show."

"No, Fitz didn't say anything about not being here. It's the first time I've gotten to the park ahead of him." He leashed up Snickers and led her out of the car.

With a grin, Zee said, "We can rub it in when he gets here." He leashed up King, gave the two dogs treats, then joined Ben, who was leaning against the car. "It's gonna be another hot one today."

"Yep," Ben replied, eyes focused toward the park entrance. "Something's not right."

"I'll second that. Ya reckon he went lookin' for Katía?"

"That's exactly what I was thinking, but where?"

Zee scratched his head. "He was mighty obsessed with that camp. I'd wager he went back there."

"That's a long ways to drive just to find out if he's there."

They lapsed into silence. Zee bent down and petted King. "You know we're gonna go, so why don't we get at it?"

"Let me call him, first." Ben pulled up Fitz in his contacts and punched dial. After four rings, it went to a message saying voicemail had not been set up. "Figures. He hasn't even set up his voicemail."

"Sounds like Fitz. So whatchya think?"

"I think I don't like this. Are you up for driving back to the camp?"

Zee's eyes sparkled. "I thought you'd never ask." After loading up the dogs, Ben pulled up directions to the park, and they were off.

*   *   *   *   *

After securing Fitz and Katía in the cave, Earl walked back to the cabin and took up his place by the door. Checking his watch, he saw it was 4:58 a.m. He saw no need to wake the others to tell them about capturing Fitz. *It'll wait till they get up.*

In the predawn darkness, he replayed the incident at the cave over and over in his mind. *I handled that like a pro, just like they would've in the movies.* As faint light peeked in the east, his thoughts snapped away from the cave to the opening of the cabin door. Earnie stepped out.

"Mornin'," Earl said.

"Mornin'. I half expected to find you asleep."

Earl stood and stretched. "We had a intruder last night."

"Oh? Was it a possum?"

"No. It was that old guy with the long beard. Came lookin' for the woman," Earl grinned.

"I assume he left without findin' 'er, but your grin's tellin' me different."

"Let's just say he's spendin' time in the cave with his girlfriend."

"How'd you get 'im in there?"

"I follered 'im. When he had the woman out of the cave, I used the shotgun to put 'em right back in. Just happened to have the duct tape with me."

Earnie scrunched up his forehead. "Now we got two in the dyin' cave. Hadn't planned on any deaths when we started this. It's all gone wrong."

"It'll be OK. We just had a wrinkle in the plan."

Earnie put his hands on his hips. "You did turn off his phone, didn't ya?"

Earl cursed under his breath and didn't answer.

"Well?"

"I didn't even think about him havin' a phone."

"Never mind. Go try to get some sleep if you want to. I'll send Everett after it while I start some coffee. The girls are still tied to the beds. Leave me the shotgun."

"Oh, yeah. I got us another pistol," he said, holding up Fitz's Beretta.

"Good. Just don't let one of them girls grab it."

"I won't."

The door opened, and Everett stepped out. "Y'all sure are chatty for this early in the mornin'."

Earnie looked to the budding sunrise. "Earl caught the old guy huntin' for the woman." He stopped and rubbed his hands through his hair. "How ya reckon he found 'er?"

"I ain't got no idea. It's like he just knew where to go. He'd stop about ever' fifty feet or so and look around and listen, … like he was divinin' 'er."

"Did he have a stick?"

"No, at least I didn't see one. Wait. No, I'm sure. He had his gun in one hand," Earl answered.

Earnie rubbed his hands through his hair again. "Everett, Earl forgot to check if the guy has a cell phone. Go see, and if the woman's still alive, leave the tape on 'er mouth. We don't need 'er fillin' your head with more talk about Mama."

Everett's lips drew thin. "I don't wanna go in a cave with no dead woman."

"She's ain't dead. I just saw 'er a little while ago, walkin' and everthang."

"You ain't lyin' are ya?" Everett asked.

Earl shook his head.

"OK, I'll go."

"Thank you can do it with one hand?" Earnie asked.

"Yeah."

"Take this with you," Earl said, handing over the Beretta.

Everett stopped at the entrance to the cave and listened. Hearing the scrape of bodies on the cave floor, he ducked and entered cautiously, Beretta at the ready. He found Katía and Fitz lying back to back about a foot apart.

Looking at Fitz, he said, "Roll on your back. I need your phone. Fitz didn't move. "Fine." Everett fished in the left front and back pockets of Fitz's jeans. "Now roll over." Fitz still didn't move. "This is your last chance," Everett said, aiming the Beretta shakily at Fitz.

Fitz stared Everett in the eyes and muttered something through the tape.

"Earnie said for me not to take the tape off. I don't wanna hear what either of you has to say. Now roll over, ... please." Fitz still didn't move, and Everett felt a drop of sweat trickling down his neck. *I have to do this. I cain't go back and tell 'em I was scared."*

He clenched his jaw and grabbed Fitz by the knees. That's when he noticed Katía's pleading eyes. "I ain't listenin' to you."

He started to roll Fitz onto his back, and Fitz jumped, grabbing Everett's arm. Surprised, he fell forward onto Fitz, reaching out with his casted hand, which also held the Beretta, to catch himself on the floor of the cave. Katía squirmed to grab for the gun. Everett was so off balance, he couldn't pull back. Having his weight on that hand caused pain to surge. The gun was pinned under his cast. Katía grabbed the cast but couldn't pull his hand off the gun.

In a panic, Everett put a knee on Fitz and jerked his cast out of Katía's grasp. The Beretta fell out of his fingers and landed about a foot from Katía's hands. As Katía squirmed madly toward the gun, Everett jerked his right hand loose from Fitz's grasp and scooped up the Beretta.

He backed away, shaking and sweating and hurting and angry. At first his rage was directed at the two captives. Then he realized he was really mad at himself. *I cain't do nothin' right. What's wrong with me? Well, I ain't gonna fail this time. I just gotta thank this through.* He scratched his beard while he pondered how to get Fitz's phone. *He might not have one. I could go and say I checked and didn't find one. That's the truth, but if he does have one, that'd be bad. I gotta do this.*

After more thought, he set the Beretta on the ground away from Fitz and Katía. "You gonna roll over or not?" Fitz still didn't move. "I ain't gonna stand for any mo' monkey business."

Kneeling down and being wary, he placed his good hand under Fitz's knee and flipped him hard. Pushing down with his knee onto Fitz's thigh, he located the phone in Fitz's back pocket and pulled it out just as Katía was squirming toward the gun.

Everett jumped up quickly, banging his head on the top of the cave. Stepping back a couple of steps, he picked up the gun and eyed the phone with satisfaction. *I did it.*

At that very moment, the phone rang. Everett jumped so hard he hit his head on the cave again and slung the phone. It landed on Katía. She squirmed to get hold of it, but Everett was faster. He snatched it up again, hitting his head a third time.

The ring tone echoed in the cave, and Everett scrambled to deny the call. Once he succeeded in silencing it, he scurried out of the cave, not trusting himself to look back. Outside, where he could stand all the way up, he rubbed the sore spots on his head. *To do this right, I'd better turn it off.*

He tried to turn off the phone but discovered it required a fingerprint or code. *Oh, no. I ain't goin' back in for his fingerprint.*

CHAPTER 35

Fitz heard Katía breathing hard and knew the effort of battling with Everett had exhausted her. She started scooting again. He wished he could tell her to save her energy. He watched, trying to tell her with his eyes. She was scooting toward him, which made his heart soften. He wanted to be close to her, too. Maybe that would help as she passed away.

When she started pivoting, bringing her feet toward his head, he was afraid she was going to kick him for not saving her. *I guess I deserve that.* He braced himself for the kick as she got closer. When her hands started exploring his face, he realized what she was up to.

Earl had wrapped the duct tape all the way around his head three times because of his beard. Katía tugged at the tape, eliciting a few ouches, which were muffled through the tape. After a few minutes and a couple of scratches on his cheek from her fingernails, his mouth was freed. Katía went limp right where she was, her breathing still hard.

"I'm sorry I didn't save you," Fitz said, a tear rolling down his cheek.

Katía muttered through her tape. Fitz understood and squirmed till he could reach the tape covering her mouth. Her tape just ran ear to ear. With effort, Fitz managed to get a fingernail under a corner and worked till he got a good grip on the tape. He winced as he started pulling, knowing the tape would hurt coming off.

He pulled slowly, hoping it would be less painful. Katía jerked her head away, and the tape ripped halfway off. "Get it over with, already."

Fitz adjusted his grip on the tape and quickly pulled it the rest of the way off.

"Thank you for coming for me. I'm sorry you're in this situation. You wouldn't be here if it weren't for me," she said.

"I'd rather be here with you than anywhere else,"

Katía laughed. "Now that's corny, but I'm glad it's you I'm with. Let's work on getting out of here."

"I don't think I can chew your tape off."

"Actually, I dropped an arrowhead when I lunged for Everett. It should be somewhere around the spot I was lying."

"That's how you got loose the first time?"

"Yeah. You're going to have to find it, though. I'm too worn out."

"You need to rest and conserve your energy." Fitz scooted till he got his hands where she thought she might have dropped the arrowhead. He squirmed around, running his hands on the floor of the cave for ten minutes before finding it. "Got it."

"Great," Katía said, her voice sounding weak. "It worked better when I sawed at the edges. Holding the tape that went around my ankles with the other hand helped with the positioning."

Katía fell silent. Fitz eyed her with concern and said, "We're going to make it out of here. Just hang in there for me." He hoped he sounded convincing.

Fitz worked till he got hold of the tape looping his ankles and found purchase with the arrowhead. He sawed frantically, trying to keep focused on the task rather than on Katía. *I have to get us out of here before it's too late for her.*

Being fresh and not dehydrated, the sawing moved more quickly. Within fifteen minutes the tape around his ankles was severed. "I'm through," he said looking to Katía, who was lying still and breathing steadily. When she didn't respond, Fitz hurried over and shook her.

"What? I'm trying to sleep here."

"Katía, I need you to stay awake. We're about to get out of here and we'll get you to a hospital."

Fitz's anxiety surged, and he cut through the tape around her ankles and wrists in a flash. Katía slept through it. Shaking her by the shoulder, he said, "Come on. Wake up, and let's get out of here. I need you to get the tape off my wrists so I can help you."

Fitz's words seemed to register, and Katía came to. Sitting up, she took the arrowhead and sawed sluggishly at the tape. Fitz tensed every muscle trying to will her to cut faster. Finally his hands were free.

"Come on."

Katía followed him out of the cave on hands and knees. Fitz helped her to her feet, wrapped her left arm around his shoulders and held her by the waist. The sun was topping the trees directly in front of the mouth of the cave.

"We're going through the woods to the road. My car's there, and I can get you to a hospital. Let's follow the sun."

"That would be a good title for a sermon," Katía said. She was leaning on Fitz, but supporting her own weight, having perked up since she got out of the cave.

Fitz started down the same hill where Katía had fled the day before, shouldering through branches and briars to try to protect Katía. She hit a steep spot and slid. Fitz reacted quickly, tightening his grip to prevent her from hitting the ground.

"If I were thirty years younger, I'd just pick you up and carry you out of here."

"My knight in shining armor."

Fitz eased his grip as she regained her footing, but she didn't move away. He adjusted his feet so they were standing face to face. He hugged her closer. "I'm so glad you're alive."

"Me, too," she said, returning the hug.

Fitz's heart flooded with warmth. He would have been happy to stay and savor that moment, but Katía was in need of medical attention. "We need to keep moving. You have to get to the hospital." They resumed the trek toward the road.

* * * * *

Everett hurried back to the cabin with Fitz's phone and presented it to Earnie.

"Did you turn it off?"

"Couldn't. Takes a code."

Earnie tried entering a couple of codes with no success. He spotted a large rock, picked it up, and smashed the phone to pieces. "That oughtta work."

"Ya reckon they'll be any more comin'," Everett asked. "Somebody called after I got it outta his pocket."

Earnie clenched his jaw. "Thangs ain't workin' out like I planned. Might have to kill the girls and leave 'em in the cave."

"We cain't kill them, too. That just ain't right. They ain't done nothin' to us like the others," Everett said. "Let's just go somewhere else. We don't need no more death."

"Where we gonna go? There ain't no place to go. This was it, I don't know nowhere else." Earnie ran his hands through his hair. "You'd better check on the girls. Make sure they ain't untyin' no ropes. … and try not to wake Earl up yet."

When Everett reached to open the cabin door, it burst open toward him, knocking him so he landed on his backside. Sadie and Laurie raced out the door and into the woods.

"Guess that answers that question," Earnie said before hollering, "Stop or I'll shoot." He ran to pick up the shotgun from the porch, but the girls didn't stop.

By the time Earnie got the gun and took aim, they had disappeared into the woods. "Well, don't just sit on your rumpus, go get 'em." Then he called for Earl. "Wake up! They's getting' away again."

"What's all the commotion?" Earl asked, leaning against the door frame.

"The girls done gone and ran off in the woods. Follow Everett. I'll go cut 'em off at the road."

Earl looked to the woods, caught sight of Everett, and loped off.

"I reckon they done earned a death sentence," Earnie growled to himself as he got into the truck.

CHAPTER 36

Sadie and Laurie had a good head start on the guys as they crashed through the woods. Sadie hoped they could outrun them because they sure couldn't be stealthy charging through the forest. She was in the lead and prayed Laurie could keep up. Their lives depended on it.

She kept charging, not daring to look back and having no idea what she was going to do if they succeeded in outrunning them. *The road must be up ahead. Maybe a car will come by.* She pushed on, hearing Laurie close behind.

Then the sound behind her changed. It sounded like Laurie fell. Torn between fleeing for her life and stopping to help, she put on the brakes and hurried back to help Laurie up. She heard the sound of another fall up the hill, then Earl's voice, "Get up, stupid."

"I hurt my wrist again," Everett whined.

"Come on, we're rurnt if they get away."

They sounded close but weren't within Sadie's sight. She scooped Laurie off the ground in an adrenaline rush and resumed fleeing. "We have to run as hard as we can," Sadie said between breaths. "It's our last chance." Laurie didn't reply but kept pace with Sadie.

Sadie caught a glimpse of a gray asphalt ribbon through the leaves and branches. *I sure hope a car is passing by.* The sight gave her renewed hope and increased her speed. Bursting out of the trees, she jumped down a four-foot bank and landed across the ditch. Laurie landed right beside her.

"Now what?" Laurie gasped.

Checking the highway in both directions, she saw a car parked on the side to her right just before the road leading to the camp. She squinted but couldn't see anyone inside. It took a moment to accept that no car was coming to their rescue. With the sounds of running coming closer, Sadie desperately searched for a place to hide. Across the road, she noticed large boulder formations rising along the steep hill. "Come on!"

Just as she started across the road, she heard an engine. Looking to her right, she saw no car on the road. "One of them is coming in the truck."

Laurie followed as Sadie scrambled up the bank and crashed into the undergrowth on the other side of the road. Her muscles burned as she battled gravity to climb the hill, searching for a hiding place.

About 200 feet up the hill, she noticed darkness to her left and stopped. She checked it out and found a recessed area that had eroded behind a huge boulder. Motioning Laurie to come, she crawled in to find a space that was approximately four feet tall, six feet deep, and six feet wide. *I hope there aren't any snakes in here.*

She and Laurie faced the front of the nook, where they could see if one of the guys looked in. Sadie held a finger to her lips, and Laurie nodded. Sadie's whole body trembled as she wondered if they would be caught. Her hope broke. *Of course they'll find us. Where else could we have gone? I won't tell Laurie that.*

Sound carried up the hill from the road, and Sadie heard the red pickup, then Earnie yelled, "You didn't catch 'em? … Well where'd they go?"

Earl replied, "I reckon someone came by and picked 'em up."

Earnie again, "Do ya see any cars? They must've crossed the road."

"There comes a car." It was Everett. Sadie had learned their voices.

"Great. Act like we lost a hubcap or somethin'." That was Earnie.

"You guys got engine trouble?" It was a voice Sadie didn't recognize. She wanted to race down to the road and plead for help but was afraid the car would pull away before they got there.

"I was a mighty fine mechanic back in the day, if I do say so myself. I might could help."

"We don't need no help. Just lost a hubcap," Earnie said.

"Maybe you could help us, then." It was another unfamiliar voice. "We're looking for a good place to fish."

"Don't fish. If ya don't mind, go on and let us get back to huntin'." That was Earl.

Sadie crawled to the opening of their little nook but couldn't see the road. She was afraid to risk coming out.

* * * * *

The going was slow. Fitz hoped the guys wouldn't come back to check on them. *What if they come back for my key so they can move the car?* The thought made him want to hurry, but Katía just didn't have it in her. She needed to stop and rest every three or four minutes to keep from passing out. Within Fitz's soul, the need to hurry battled with the drive to care for her.

They stopped to rest again. Katía sat on a large rock. Fitz scanned the woods, looking for the road and signs of pursuers. Adrenaline caused his heart to race.

"I'm not sure I can keep going," Katía said, her voice a whisper.

"We have to keep going. The road has to be close by. My car's there, and we can get you to the hospital.

"I'm just so tired, Fitz."

He stood close and rubbed her back. "We're going to make it. You have to keep fighting."

"I would if I could."

A sound registered in Fitz's mind. At first he had assumed it was the breeze, but now it sounded like water: a creek. "Do you hear that?" he asked with excitement.

"All I hear is my heart beating and my ears ringing."

"It's a creek, and it's not too far away. Come on, let's get you some water." He helped her to her feet.

"You realize it's not a good idea to drink from a creek anymore, right?"

"It beats dying from dehydration," he replied, wrapped her arm around his neck, and held tightly to her waist.

"If I don't make it, just know that this is nice, being close like this."

"I think you're getting delirious."

Fitz slowly marched her through the woods, now supporting over half of her weight. Katía's knees buckled, and Fitz had to let her down for another rest. They had hardly walked a minute. The creek didn't sound any closer.

What if it's just a breeze? He looked down at Katía. She sat propped up against his leg. If he moved, she'd fall over. "We need to rest for a while." He gently laid her on her back and sat beside her.

Without opening her eyes, she said, "Don't just leave my body out in the woods for critters to eat."

Fitz stiffened. "Don't talk like that. You're not going to die."

"Just promise me."

"OK, I promise, but you'd better not die while I'm trying to save you. That won't look good at all."

One corner of her mouth moved up into a slight smile. Then she was asleep. At first Fitz feared the worst, but her steady breathing showed she was still alive. He pulled his knees up, wrapped his arms around them, and tried to figure out what to do.

The idea that made the most sense was just too painful to execute. *I should go get the car and bring back an ambulance. I just can't bear to leave her. What if she dies before I get back? No, I'll let her sleep a few minutes then we'll try again. What if she doesn't wake up? Maybe I should go for help. I wish I'd brought M&Ms.*

With his mind running in circles and his heart struggling with the strain, Fitz finally decided that waiting and trying again after a few minutes was his best option. *I could go find the creek and see what it looks like.*

Working his way back onto his feet took a couple of groans, then he set off in the direction that he believed led to the road. He looked back frequently to check on Katía until he could no longer see her. The sound of the creek moved to his left as he proceeded. When he glimpsed the highway through the leaves, he realized they wouldn't cross the creek. *I have water in the car, and it's closer. We have to make it to the road.*

A surge of concern propelled Fitz back to Katía. He found her sleeping peacefully. The curve of her eyelids stirred something in Fitz's heart that he hadn't felt since before he lost Sharon. He sat and watched her, letting his heart warm.

Then anxiety hit like a hammer. Feeling that he was betraying Sharon's memory collided with the need to get Katía to a hospital. The dream where Sharon was lying in the coffin and woke up to tell him it was OK to move on flashed in his mind. *I'll deal with all that later. I have to get Katía moving.*

He gently shook her shoulder. "Wake up. The highway is not too far off. I found it." She didn't awaken, so he shook a little harder and repeated himself, trying to keep the flash of worry out of his voice.

"Come on, Katía, you have to wake up!"

CHAPTER 37

Fitz didn't want to yell, fearing he would alert the Inmanson boys. Instead of shaking her shoulder, he tried patting Katía's thigh to awaken her. Finally her eyes opened halfway.

"I was sleeping so good and dreaming about swimming in a lake. The water felt wonderful and there were otters swimming along with me. I wish you'd let me finish the dream."

Then a look of confusion came over her, and she rolled onto one elbow. "Where am I? What are we doing in the woods? Oh, no! Now I remember. That's why I'm still tired."

Fitz helped her sit up. "The highway isn't too far away. Let's see if we can get you there."

"OK. I'll try."

Fitz got behind her, put his arms under hers, and lifted her onto her feet.

"Thanks," she said.

"You're welcome. Now let's take it slow and easy and see how far we can get." He helped support her and off they went.

"You probably should have left me and gone for help," she said.

"I thought about it, but I just couldn't."

Katía squeezed a little hug with the arm wrapped around his neck. He returned the gesture.

After two more rests, a streak of asphalt appeared through the leaves. Fitz stopped when he heard voices. It was the Inmansons, and it sounded like they were looking for the girls. He eased Katía down so he could get a closer look.

Moving toward the road, he found a tree trunk behind which he could hide. Leaning out just enough, he was able to make out the red truck. Then a white Outback pulled up, and he heard Zee's voice. He caught himself just before he jumped out and yelled to Ben for help. *They have a shotgun and two pistols.* He forced himself to wait when all his being yearned to get help for Katía.

Ben and Zee drove off. *They'll be back.* The Inmansons lingered, looking across the road.

"I reckon they either got picked up or kept goin' across the road," one of them said.

"I don't hear 'em, so it's more likely they got picked up."

"Could be hidin'. Thank we oughter look?"

"Couldn't hurt. If we cain't find 'em, we gotta get outta here. I'll stay here in case they come out to flag a car."

Fitz saw two of the guys disappear into the woods across the road.

"What's happening?" Katía asked.

Fitz turned and put a finger to his lips. *If the other one would just go with them, I could try to get to the car.* Waiting was hard. He crept back to Katía, surprised she was still awake and sitting right where he had left her. He sat beside her.

"I think the girls got away," he whispered into her ear.

She squirmed. "Your beard tickles," she whispered back. "I hope they don't catch them. They got punched in the face last time."

Time forgot to move as Fitz sat waiting for the truck to leave. Katía leaned into him, and her head lolled over. Fitz braced himself to hold her up. *Maybe another nap will help.* He checked to make sure she was still breathing.

Fitz thought his nerves were going to catch fire before he heard the truck crank. It turned around in the road and drove off. Fitz laid Katía down and hurried to the edge of the woods, getting there just in time to see the truck turn up the camp road. His car was right where he'd left it, though it had a bright sticker on it from law enforcement.

Fitz ran to the car, whipped it around in the road and drove back to where he had left Katía. When he got back to her, she was still sleeping.

"Come on. One more time. Wake up, Katía!"

Her eyes fluttered open.

"My car's right here. Buffett's ready to see you. Come on."

Without waiting for her to initiate, he pulled her into sitting, then into standing. Supporting three fourths of her weight now, he helped her till they reached the bank, which was a four-foot drop-off. He stopped, puzzling how to get her down. Her knees buckled, and he helped her to the ground.

"Let me sit here, and you get down, then slide me down," She murmured.

Fitz scrambled down the bank, got in front of her, pulled her to him and eased her down. He tried to move to her side, but she didn't let go. She smiled.

"Fitz Fitzgerald, you saved me," she said, hugging him tightly.

He squeezed her, then said, "Not yet. We have to get to the hospital before you're really saved."

"OK, if you insist. Wouldn't it be nice to have a picnic here? We could set out a blanket and enjoy the view. Isn't the lake pretty?"

"What lake? Oh, no, you're seeing things. We have to hurry." Fitz dragged her to the car and maneuvered her into the front seat. "Look who I found, Buffett."

He stopped at the back and got two bottles of water. Opening one for Katía, he said, "Drink it slowly. Otherwise it might make you sick."

Katía took a long drink.

"Whoa, there." He pulled the bottle down from her mouth. "Let that settle." He jumped out and got two more bottles just in case.

"I wonder where the hospital is?" Checking on Katía's progress, he discovered the bottle was empty. He drank half of his before offering Katía a second bottle. "Slow down on this one."

As Fitz reached to start the car, the red truck pulled onto the highway. "Get down!" They leaned toward the center of the car, bumping heads before getting lower than the dashboard.

Fitz heard the truck engine fade, so he looked out. It was headed back into town.

"We have to follow them," Katía urged. "Go before you lose them!"

Fitz cranked the car, puzzled that Katía was making sense again. "I guess the water helped." He pulled onto the road.

"What do you mean?"

"You were seeing things just a minute ago."

"No I wasn't."

Fitz decided there was no use in arguing as he accelerated toward the truck. With his brow knitted, he tried to keep far enough behind the truck not to be noticed but close enough to see if it made a turn.

As he drove, his heart was at war. *I can't follow them. I have to get Katía to the hospital. Her life might depend on it. But water is probably what she needs most, and she has that. If the girls got away, then it doesn't matter if I follow the truck. I should go to the hospital.*

"Why do you look so worried?" Katía broke in.

Fitz didn't want to tell her what he was thinking. The weakness in her voice sealed his decision. "We can't follow them. I want to get you to the hospital."

"Are you crazy? I'll be fine. We can't let them get away."

Fitz scrunched his eyebrows together, trying to make sense out of the demands competing in his heart. "I think the girls got away. Rescuing you and them is what really mattered. I'm more concerned about you than catching the guys."

"That's sweet but follow them. If they get away, they'll probably just kidnap more girls."

A blare of sirens caught Fitz's attention. Blue lights strobed from three cars in a line headed their way. "Ben and Zee must have called the police."

CHAPTER 38

Zee craned his neck, looking back as Ben drove away from the guys standing beside the red truck on the side of the road. "Where you think those girls are?"

"I don't know. The way the guys are just standing beside the road seems odd. I wonder if the girls got away." Ben mused.

"Don't know, but Fitz and Katía aren't with them either. Surely they ain't gone and killed 'em all."

"I don't think so. If they had, why would they be standing around like that? If I'd killed four people, I'd be hightailing it out of here."

"You don't reckon the truck really broke down, do you?" Zee asked.

Ben thought for a beat. "I think it's more likely somebody got away and they were hunting for them. Whether it was the girls or Fitz and Katía is a toss of the dice."

"Wouldn't they have left somebody back to keep an eye on the others?" Zee wondered.

"If they're hogtied like Katía was in the back of the truck, then they wouldn't be worried about their getting away," Ben replied.

"Now what we gonna do?" Zee asked.

"I'd say call 911 first. Got your phone?"

Zee placed the call, described what was going on, and gave them their approximate location.

Waiting till an oncoming car passed, Ben turned around. "Let's go back and pretend we're lost. Asking for directions again ought to really irritate them."

"You remember they have guns, right?"

"Yep. Hold this just in case," Ben said, sliding the pistol out of its holster.

"Thanks."

When they got back to where the road leading to the camp turned off, Ben stopped and puzzled. "Fitz's car is gone."

"So are the guys," Zee added.

Ben scratched his head. "Did they leave or go back to the camp?"

"They might have come just to get Fitz's car."

"That makes sense, but why did all three come?"

"They like to stick together? I don't know. Don't look good for Fitz, though."

"We'd better get to that camp in a hurry. You want to walk or drive in and play stupid?" Ben asked.

"My knee says it'd rather play stupid."

Ben pulled onto the old camp road and approached the parking area cautiously.

"I don't see the truck or Fitz's car," Zee said.

"That's weird. Maybe they hid them behind a building."

"Don't tell me we're gettin' out to check," Zee said.

"I don't know any other way to find out. Let me holster the gun so it doesn't look like we're coming in shooting."

Zee handed the pistol back to Ben. "Be ready to pull it out, though."

"Try to look lost and confused," Ben suggested.

"That won't be hard 'cause that's exactly what I am."

Ben looked around, scratching his head and trying to act like he was lost. When nobody came out, he motioned Zee to follow and hurried to the side of the old dining hall building.

Zee caught up to him, and Ben led the way to the back. Finding nothing there, he worked his way through the woods to the backs of the cabins, peeking in the windows as he went.

"Ain't nobody here," Zee observed.

They walked to the front of the cabins and found a cellphone on the ground, smashed.

"That looks like Fitz's," Ben said, stooping to pick it up.

"Better just leave it there. This is a crime scene, and the police won't take kindly to us messin' with it," Zee pointed out.

As if on cue, the sound of sirens reached the camp. "I hope they figure out to come on up here," Zee said.

A couple of minutes later, they could see the first deputy's car approaching the parking area, followed by two more.

"How we gonna do this without gettin' shot?" Zee asked.

"We're the good guys, remember."

"Yeah, but they don't know that. You might oughtta do somethin' with that gun."

"Come on, let's go so they don't think we're hiding."

"OK, but I'm stayin' behind you," Zee said, following Ben.

As they approached, the deputies drew their guns and yelled for Ben and Zee to put their hands on their heads. They complied, and Ben led the way into the open.

One of the deputies yelled, "He has a weapon! On your knees!"

Ben complied, then heard a deputy yell, "I said on your knees!"

"I'm workin' on it," Zee said. "Ole Arthur's makin it a bit tricky."

With Zee finally down, one of the deputies relieved Ben of his gun, then patted them down.

"We're the ones who called you," Ben said. "It looks like the kidnappers left."

"Are you people crazy?" one of the deputies said. "You could have gotten yourselves killed."

"I'm aware of that, but they have two friends of ours as well as two teenage girls," Ben replied.

"I'm Deputy Carlson, and we appreciate your concern, but where are they? Was this a hoax?" He was brown-haired, clean shaven, and a thick bear of a man.

Ben took a breath to squelch his anger. "This was definitely no hoax. We're talking about the men in the red Chevy truck you received an APB on. We saw them on the road and assume this is where they were hiding. It appears they got away. There's evidence they were holed up in that cabin." He pointed.

"Brad and Joe, take their statements separately. I'll go have a look," Deputy Carlson said. Brad and Joe were young, thin, and could have been brothers.

Brad led Ben to the porch of the dining hall.

"First thing," Ben said, "You need to alert the rest of the deputies to be on the lookout for that red truck."

Brad rolled his eyes. "We're already watching for it. Now tell me the story, starting at the beginning."

Just after Ben began telling the story, Deputy Carlson came back for a camera. "There's definitely been someone holing up here, and I found a smashed cell phone."

"I think that smashed phone belongs to my friend Fitz," Ben offered.

"I'm starting to believe your crazy story," Deputy Carlson replied. "If all you saw were the three young men at the truck, where are their prisoners?"

Ben put both hands on his head. "I wish I knew. I hope they didn't kill them before they left. If they had, I don't think they would have been standing around in the road the way they were."

"Unless they were looking for a piece of incriminating evidence," Brad suggested.

Deputy Carlson returned to the cabin while Brad continued the interview. Ben told everything he could remember, starting with locating the note in the bottle at Laurel Park. "After we called 911, we decided to drive back by to see if they were still there. The truck and Fitz's car were both gone. You probably passed them on your way here."

"I wish I'd realized that was them."

CHAPTER 39

Buffett had curled up in Katía's lap, and his purr filled the car. Katía punched Fitz in the shoulder. "It's sweet that you're worried about me, but I'll be fine. Fluid is all I needed … and maybe a little food. Don't you dare let them get away."

Fitz noted the seriousness of Katía's expression as he followed the Inmanson's truck.

"I'm serious," she continued. "Could you live with yourself if they kidnap another girl?"

Fitz clenched his jaw as he considered what she'd said. "This is impossible."

"It's not impossible Fitz. Just follow the truck. I'll make you a promise. If I start feeling bad again, I'll tell you and willingly go to the hospital." She squirmed in her seat.

Fitz caught the movement in the corner of his eye. "See, you're hurting."

"Being sore from lying on rocks won't kill me. It'll hurt worse if you let that truck get away."

Fitz melted under the sincerity of her gaze. "OK, but if you die on me, I'm going to kill you. There are some granola bars in the glove box."

Katía pulled two out, opened one, and handed it to Fitz. "This is delicious," she said after her first bite.

"They're especially tasty when you're starving," Fitz added.

Fitz followed the truck into and through the town of Toccoa. He felt sure Katía had to be exhausted. "Feel free to take a nap. It looks like this is going to be a long ride," he said as he followed them onto a four-lane highway.

"I sure am glad to be out of that cave, though I did have a lot of time to pray."

"It looks like God answered your prayers."

"I was expecting to be in heaven by now and felt like God would get me through the ordeal," she said.

"Sorry, but I don't think this is even close," Fitz chuckled.

"I don't know. I have a cat in my lap, you beside me, and I'm alive."

Fitz could feel his cheeks flushing. "They wouldn't go back to the farm, would they? The truck's headed in that direction."

"That would be crazy," Katía said. "I bet they turn north when they get to three-sixty-five and go to North Carolina."

"You're probably right," Fitz replied. "I wish they'd stop for coffee."

Katía chuckled. "Are you in coffee withdrawal already?"

"Not yet, but it's coming."

They had driven a little farther, then Fitz exclaimed, "No! Oh, buzzard breath."

"What is it?"

"I'm about to run out of gas."

*   *   *   *   *

"When you finish taking statements, go check out the cabin and make sure I didn't miss anything," Deputy Carlson requested as he returned from photographing and bagging potential evidence.

"That's quite a haul," Brad said, eyeing the many bags in the deputy's hands.

"Yeah, they left a nice mess."

"I think we need to search the grounds to make sure the girls or our friends aren't here," Ben suggested.

"I hope they ain't here 'cause if they are, it won't be good," Zee said.

Brad and Joe surveyed the cabin and surrounding grounds, coming back with a lighter and two cigarette butts Deputy Carlson had missed. They had also looked through the other cabins.

"Found a latrine behind one of 'em," Joe said. "I guess we ought to photograph that, too."

Deputy Carlson handed Joe the camera. "You do the honors, then let's spread out in a search grid and walk the grounds." He asked Ben and Zee, "You guys wanna help?"

"Of course," Ben replied.

They fanned out and moved north, with Ben ending up on the trail they had followed the day before.

* * * * *

"I can't stand it any longer," Sadie said. "I have to see if they're still there."

Laurie nodded, then Sadie led the way out of their hiding place, jumping to the ground when a twig cracked. It was so loud in the silence. Laurie followed suit.

Realizing what had happened, Sadie whispered, "Sorry, it was just a stick." She resumed moving and found a spot from which they could see the road. It was empty. "The truck's gone," she said with disbelief.

"The car that was parked on the side of the road's gone, too," Laurie observed.

The peal of sirens caused Sadie to duck. Laurie ducked too, then said, "A police car! Maybe we can flag them down."

Wondering why she had ducked, Sadie scrambled down the hill toward the road. Before they could get out of the woods and onto the shoulder of the road, three sheriff's cars screamed by and turned up the camp road.

"That's good," Laurie said. "I hope they shoot those guys."

Despite the urge to race after the cars, Sadie stayed put. "You're right. There might be a shootout. I think we should wait here till they come back out." She sat on a nearby boulder.

"Do you think we're ever going to get back home?" Laurie asked, hands dropping to her side.

Sadie reached out, and Laurie took her hand. "It's almost over. We will definitely be able to get those deputies' attention when they come back. Sit down and as soon as we hear cars coming, we'll run out to the road."

"What if it's the bad guys? What if they shoot all of the deputies and run?"

She squeezed Laurie's hand. "Don't think like that. We're going to be safe."

Sadie struggled with waiting. Her heart kept pushing to go find the deputies. Finally, she could stand it no longer. "I don't hear any gunshots. Let's go."

Laurie nodded and followed as Sadie led the way.

"I'm going up the road so we don't miss them if they leave."

Keeping close to the side of the road, nerves on high alert, Sadie made her way quickly toward the camp. As she approached, she heard voices but couldn't make out what they were saying. Stopping to listen closer, she still couldn't make it out. She looked to Laurie, who shrugged her shoulders.

Sadie could tell from the tone that the voices didn't sound angry. Then they faded and disappeared. Puzzled, she resumed walking toward the camp. As she approached the parking area, she saw the three deputy cars and a white Outback.

"Where did they go?" Sadie asked.

"Maybe they're inside," Laurie suggested.

Sadie entered the dining hall with Laurie in tow. A quick search showed no one there.

"Let's try the cabins," Sadie suggested.

They peeked into the cabins. Sadie shuddered when she opened the door to the one in which they had been trapped. After searching the last cabin, she put her hands on her hips. "Where could they have gone?"

"Maybe they're searching for us," Laurie replied. "Let's wait near the cars to make sure they can't leave without us."

"I want to go to the cave and check on Katía. I hope she's not ..." Sadie trailed off.

"Dead, you mean?"

"Yeah."

"What if they leave while we're at the cave?"

"That's not good. Why don't you wait near the cars, and I'll go to the cave ... not that I'm excited to find a dead body."

Noting the fear etched on Laurie's face, Sadie added, "It'll be OK. The bad guys are gone."

"OK."

"I'll hurry. … Hide if you here a car coming up the road." While Laurie walked toward the cars, Sadie hurried down the path toward the cave.

Nearing the cave, Sadie heard twigs cracking and leaves rustling to each side of the trail. She froze, her first thought being that the Inmansnons had been hiding in the woods. The sounds were moving away instead of toward her, prompting her second thought: *Bears.*

It finally dawned on her that she might be hearing the deputies. That hope released her feet, and she began walking cautiously but quickly. Then the drive to feel safe pushed her to run. She rounded a curve in the trail and ran right into Ben.

He had turned at the approaching sound. When his arms wrapped around Sadie to prevent her falling, she jerked away.

"It's OK, Sadie. We're trying to help you," Ben said.

Sadie's hands flew to her face. The terror of the last few weeks escaped, rolling down her cheeks in liquid form.

"You're going to be safe," Ben added. "Do you know where the others are?"

"Laurie's back by the cars. We didn't want y'all to leave without us," Sadie whimpered. "They tied up a woman named Katía in a cave and left her to die. I was coming to see if she's … I hope she's still alive."

Zee and the deputies had converged on Sadie and Ben. Ben asked, "Can you take me to the cave?"

"Come on," Sadie said and took off at a sprint. After another hundred yards, she stopped and looked around, waiting for Ben and the deputies to catch up. "We turned off the trail somewhere around here."

Ben went a little farther, then called, "I've got something here."

The others gathered around pieces of duct tape lying on the ground.

"The cave's that way," Sadie said, pointing. "I'd rather one of you check."

Ben hurried to the entrance of the cave calling, "Katía! Fitz!" Hearing no sound, he turned on the flashlight on his phone and entered the cave. "More duct tape, but nobody's in here."

"Brad, escort this young lady and these two gentlemen back to the cars and make sure the other girl is safe. Joe and I'll process this scene," Deputy Carlson ordered. "Hurry, just in case those creeps come back."

CHAPTER 40

Fitz slammed his hands on the steering wheel, then turned into the gas station. "I can't believe this. If only I'd gassed up on the way, but I was in too much of a hurry to find you."

"Blame it on me, that's OK," Katía deadpanned.

Fitz filled the car with gas, then asked, "Do you want anything besides water and granola bars?"

Katía opened her door. "It may not be the best, but at least they'll have coffee."

"I could use some of that, too. I think this is a sign that I need to get you to the hospital."

"It could be, but I don't sense that it is. Let's grab coffee and keep going."

"Keep going where?" Fitz asked. "We don't know where they're headed.

Katía grinned. "I think I do."

"And just how could you know where they're going," he asked while opening the door for her.

"Someone needs to tend to their cows."

"Brilliant! I bet you're right."

Katía grinned again. "I'd pay, but I left my purse in my car."

Fitz chuckled. "I'm happy to buy your coffee."

Pulling out onto the road, Fitz headed toward the Inmansons' farm.

"We should have asked the clerk at the store to call the sheriff's office and alert them," Katía said.

"Hind sight's twenty-twenty."

"I hope you still have some extra Berettas. I don't feel comfortable going after them with a stick."

"I have three more back there, so we should be good."

"One for Buffett, too," Katía laughed. "Can you handle a gun?" she asked Buffett, who had retaken his spot in her lap.

"Meow."

"He thinks he can, anyway," Fitz laughed. "How are you feeling after a few sips of coffee?"

"I won't lie. I'm worn out. That was quite an ordeal, but I don't feel I'm at death's door like I did earlier."

"I think we should go to the hospital and call the deputies from there."

"No, they might feed the cows and run. I don't want these creeps to get away, Fitz. I just wish we had our phones." She reached over and rubbed Fitz's shoulder. "I'm going to be all right."

Katía's touch felt warm, and the warmth lingered after she moved her hand away. Fitz was puzzled by the wish that she would touch him again. "You'd better be all right."

Fitz banished the odd feeling by focusing on what they would do when they got to the farm. "I'm going to block the driveway with the car so they can't escape. I hope they'll put down the guns. A shootout's the last thing we need."

"What if they keep the guns with them?" Katía asked. "Maybe we should let them have an escape route. I'd rather they get away than anyone get shot."

"They're not getting away again. But what if they're not there?" Fitz wondered.

"That would mean I was wrong."

Fitz parked at an angle in the middle of the Inmansons' driveway, stopping before he could see the house. "Stay put, Buffett. We'll be back soon," he instructed the cat after pulling out two Berettas and ammo from the lock box. "Do you think they'll be in the house or the barn?"

"If they came to tend to the cows, I'd guess the barn," Katía said.

Fitz touched her arm, "Be careful. If you start feeling bad, just hide somewhere."

"Aww, I think you're concerned about me."

Fitz sputtered, "If... let's go through the woods to the side of the house, then to the barn. That will give us maximum cover."

"What if they're in the house?"

"You said they'd be in the barn."

"Yeah, but that's just a guess."

"Come on."

They scrambled through the woods till they were even with the house. Fitz saw no sign of the goons or the truck. "Let's go a little farther so we can see the barn." There was still no sign of the truck.

"Look," Katía pointed. The cows were moseying toward the back of the barn. "They do that when someone comes to feed them," she whispered.

"Let's cross to the house. Stay close to it when we get there."

"Yes, sir," Katía saluted and grinned.

Fitz shook his head, moved to the edge of the woods, crouched, and led the way across the yard to the house.

Standing next to the house underneath the kitchen window, Fitz heard movement inside. Katía pointed toward the window and whispered, "What do we do now?"

Fitz worked through the options and risks in his mind. *If we go to the barn, whoever's in the house could see us. If we enter the house, whoever's in the barn could hear the ruckus.*

"Hey, Everett. Don't forget them sleepin' bags," sounded through the window.

"Gettin' 'em now."

Katía whispered, "They're going to feed the cows, then hide out in the woods somewhere."

"Our best move might be to try to shoot out the tires when they're leaving. Then we'd have them all contained in the truck," Fitz suggested.

"What if we miss?"

"They'd probably stop and come after us. We'd still have them in one spot."

"But where's the truck?"

Fitz thought a beat. "It has to be behind the barn," he whispered back. He tried to come up with an option that wouldn't end up in a shootout with the risk of Katía's being hit, or worse, killed. Now he wished he hadn't brought her here. "I don't like this. Let's see if we can get back to the car and wait for them."

Katía's hands went to her hips and her eyebrows scrunched together. Fitz could sense an argument coming. The building anger morphed into a grin. "You're afraid I'll get hurt. I can take care of myself, Fitz. Besides, these guys have probably never shot a pistol in their lives. Just watch out for the shotgun. I say we go to the barn and take the lone guy first. If the ones in the house see us, we'll have cover when they come."

Fitz couldn't argue with her logic, even though waiting in the car felt safer. "Ok, but do you think you have the energy to run?"

"We'll find out. See if you can keep up."

Katía moved to the corner, scanned the barn, then took off. Fitz wasn't expecting her to break for the barn so suddenly. Caught by surprise, he was several steps behind as they crossed the yard.

Moving to the open front of the barn, Fitz could hear one of the guys talking, apparently to the cows.

"Come and get it! Breakfast is served."

Fitz could also hear water running. Putting a finger to his lips, he looked inside the barn. He saw Earl spreading hay about a hundred feet out from the back of the barn. The shotgun was propped on a bale nearby. Fitz entered the barn and crossed to the opposite side, out of Earl's line of sight.

He checked the ground ahead for obstacles, then started toward the back. He froze at the sound of the house door opening.

CHAPTER 41

Fitz felt the adrenaline surge as he tried to work out what to do. *Did the door open because they saw us? Are they both coming? I have to assume so.* Within a split second, he decided what he had to do.

He motioned to Katía to get into the first stall and to keep an eye on who was coming from the house. He pointed to his chest, then toward Earl. Katía nodded, then they moved toward their targets.

Fitz stayed near the wall till he got to the back of the barn. Without hesitation he hurried out, Beretta in hand. Two cows' eyes bulged as they shied away from the hay Earl was scattering, prompting Earl to look in Fitz's direction.

When Earl eyed the shotgun, Fitz said, "Don't you dare. Hands on your head and get in the barn." He collected the shotgun and followed Earl into the barn. "Into the far stall."

They joined Katía in the stall, Fitz pulling the door to just as he saw Earnie peek into the barn. "Get in the corner and don't move," Fitz growled to Earl.

"Come out with your hands up or I start shootin'," Earnie yelled.

"Go ahead and shoot. Your brother's standing right in front of the door." He pushed Katía to the front wall of the barn. "If you surrender, I won't shoot Earl."

"You ain't got Earl, so come on out and let's talk this over."

"No, thank you. I've seen how you treat company," Fitz called back. "Earl, let your brother know you're in here."

Earl glared at Fitz as though he could shoot poison darts with his eyes. "I'm here."

"Dang, Earl, why'd you go an' get caught?"

"Those two's s'posed ta be dead," Fitz heard Everett whisper. "Ya reckon they're zombies?"

"You're not going to risk your brother's life, are you?" Fitz said. "I can definitely kill him before you get in here. I might be able to take out all three of you. It's not worth that, is it?"

While Fitz was focused on trying to talk Earnie down, the report of Katía's pistol startled him. She yelled, "Don't move!"

Glancing at Earl, he saw he was nearly on his feet. He sat back down in a hurry, eyes wide. Fitz braced himself, wondering if Earnie would storm the stall.

Katía called out, "Everett, your brother's still alive for now. I won't miss next time. You know that what your brothers are doing is evil and your mama would be very mad about all of this. You need to help him see what's right."

"Shut up!" Earnie yelled. Then Fitz heard him say, "Don't listen to 'er. She didn't even know Mama. How could she know what Mama'd thank.?"

Whispering followed, and Fitz couldn't make out what Earnie was saying. He tensed, fearing they were planning an attack. Scanning the stall, he discovered it was open to a loft above. He motioned for Katía to get down and keep an eye on Earl. He went to the back corner so he could see farther into the loft.

When boards creaked from the above, Katía rushed out of the stall. "What are you doing?" Fitz wanted to go after her but needed to guard Earl and be ready for the attack from the loft.

He heard Katía say in a soothing voice, "Put the gun down, Everett. You know your mama wouldn't want you to shoot anyone. Come on, be a nice Christian boy like she'd want you to be."

In the tense silence, Earnie's head appeared in the loft. Fitz fired a warning shot, and Earnie scurried back, then called, "Shoot 'er, Everett! We're all dependin' on ya!"

Hearing creaks moving back toward the ladder, Fitz moved to the door. As he reached for it, it popped open, and Katía hurried Everett inside.

"Everett, you idiot! You've ruined ever'thang!" Earl screeched.

"You gonna get disciplined when this is all over, Everett," Earnie yelled.

Fitz was torn between wanting to scream at Katía for doing such a risky thing and praising her for getting Everett subdued. He kept his eyes trained on the loft. "I don't think your brother's too happy with you, Everett. He might shoot you himself. You'd better keep away from the door."

Everett looked like a crazed raccoon, rubbing his hands through his hair wildly. "What've I done? What've I done? I let my brothers down."

"It's OK, Everett. Your mama would be proud of you for doing the right thing, even if your brothers don't like it," Katía soothed. "Let's do like Fitz said and sit down near this wall."

Fitz heard the creak of the ladder. "He's coming down. I can get him while he's on the ladder," he whispered. He cracked the door open to look, and a shot rang out. Jumping back, he said, "Guess not."

Fitz could hear Earnie scurrying around in the barn. The tractor chugged to life. "Is he going to ram the door?"

"I don't know. It sounds like it's moving out of the barn."

"Earnie wouldn't tear up the barn," Everett said. "Mama taught us to take care of things around the farm."

"She must have been a good mama," Katía replied.

"Shut up, Everett. You know Daddy beat that stuff into us. It weren't Mama," Earl scolded.

"I'm purdy sure it was Mama. Daddy spent all his time workin'."

"Yeah, when he weren't beatin' us," Earl countered.

The tractor engine shut off. It sounded like it was near the house. Fitz opened the door to look but couldn't see Earnie. He started out, planning to ambush Earnie when he heard a scrape from the corner near Earl.

"On the ground or you're losing a leg," Fitz ordered Earl, who had started to stand again. *I can't risk going after him. They might overpower Katía.* He closed the door, his instincts pushing him to go out while he had the advantage.

He asked Katía, "Can you shoot them if they try to get you?"

"I'd be happy to since they've treated me so badly," she replied.

"OK. I'm going out to ambush him." He opened the door and was halfway out when a gunshot sounded and the wood splintered just above his head. Jumping back inside, he said, "I'm lucky he's not a good shot."

"We ain't never had no pistols, but we're good with the shotgun. It helps keep coyotes out."

"Shut up, Everett!"

"Quit tellin' me to shut up. I'm just tellin' the truth," Everett protested.

"Everthin' you say is makin' it harder for Earnie to rescue us," Earl replied.

"What do you think Earnie will do next, Everett?" Katía asked softly.

"I don't know, ma'am."

Earl had a fierce scowl on his face, which apparently prompted Everett to add, "And if I did know, I wouldn't tell ya."

Fitz tugged his beard. "Whatever he's doing, I'm sure it has something to do with flushing us out of here."

CHAPTER 42

The silence pounded Fitz's nerves as he waited in the barn. He hated not knowing what was coming. Finally, he asked Katía, "Got any ideas?"

"Whatever he's up to, I'm sure he's not going to hurt his brothers," she answered.

"Earnie wouldn't hurt us," Everett confirmed.

"We're at a stalemate. He can't come in, and we can't go out." Fitz froze at mid tug on his beard.

"What is it, Fitz?" Katía asked.

"I know what I'd do if I were in his place: burn down the barn."

"Are you nuts? He won't do that with his brothers in here," Katía countered.

"It would force us all out. I assume he's hoping we won't kill them before we flee."

"Earnie ain't gonna burn the barn down. We need it," Everett added.

The sound of sloshing against the wall suggested Everett was wrong.

"Don't do it, Earnie," Earl yelled. "This un's been in the cave too long, and she's startin' to fade. They'll have to come out to get 'er some help. Just wait 'em out."

Fitz hadn't thought about Katía's physical condition since they had gotten trapped in the barn. He studied her eyes and saw weariness.

"I'm fine. Don't listen to him," she whispered.

Fitz tugged his beard harder. "Is there anything else in the barn that's valuable?" he asked Everett.

"Hay and fuel for the tractor."

"How much fuel?" Fitz asked, a new concern constricting his chest.

"About fifty gallons."

"Everett, if you don't shut up, I'm gonna kill you when this is done," Earl growled.

Fitz turned to Katía. "If he lights a fire, we have to get out before the fuel explodes. We're going out with one of them in front of each of us so he'll have to shoot them first. You take Everett, and I'll take this scumbag."

"Got it," Katía answered.

"Everett, you gotta get away from 'er so Earnie can shoot 'er. They's tryin' ta take the farm away from us, understand?"

Everett nodded his head.

"You'll both die if you try to get away," Fitz growled. "I'll be sure to shoot you before he can shoot me. Since he's a bad shot, you know that's the truth."

The puff of igniting diesel grabbed Fitz's attention. A minute later, wood began to crackle, and smoke seeped into the stall.

"You're not such hotshots now, are ya?" Earnie yelled.

"What have you done?" Everett yelled back.

"Shut up, Everett. It's fer your own good," Earnie answered.

Fitz noticed fear register in Katía's eyes. "How long do we wait?"

"Let the smoke get going strong. I hope it'll cloud his vision," Fitz replied.

"It'll cloud ours, too."

Fitz scrunched his eyebrows together, then responded, "Yeah, but we don't have to worry about shooting family." He could feel the heat coming through the boards.

Everett's eyes were wide. "We gotta get outta here before we burn up! I'm leavin'. Shoot me if you wanna. Come on, Earl!" He bolted for the door.

Fitz lunged, grabbed the back of his shirt, and yanked him back into the stall.

"I think he's right, Fitz," Katía said. "It's time to go."

"OK. I don't know if he's at the front or back of the barn. Let me have a look." Fitz pulled open the door and stuck his head out. Smoke was billowing past the front of the barn, obscuring his sight. Looking to the back, he didn't see Earnie. "I don't see him."

"They's getting' ready to run," Earl yelled. He had moved away from the back wall where the fire had started but was still on the ground.

Fitz's blood boiled. He was tempted to shoot Earl right then to keep him from putting them at more of a disadvantage. He couldn't bear putting Katía in any more danger. Realizing that if he did shoot Earl, he wouldn't have a shield when they left the stall was the only thing that stopped him.

"Come on, Fitz. I don't want to die in here," Katía urged.

Smoke had gathered above the stall and was drifting down. Fitz knew they had to move. "Hold the back of his shirt and don't let go. Keep your gun aimed at his head until you see Earnie. If you see him before I do, you have to shoot."

"Got it," she responded. "Do you think he'll really shoot Everett?"

"I hope not," Fitz answered. "Get up!" he directed Earl. Earl leaned back against the wall and grinned. In no mood for games, Fitz fired a warning shot, hitting the wall just above Earl's head. "I'm not asking again."

Grabbing the back of Earl's shirt, Fitz shoved him to the door. "Got any hunch as to whether we should go toward the front or back?"

"I like the front. It's closer. Plus, we could get lost in the smoke," Katía answered.

"The front it is, then." Ensuring his grip on Earl's shirt was secure, he heard a loud voice as he reached for the door: "Don't move! Drop the gun!"

Confusion squirreled around in Fitz's mind. He looked at Katía. "Ben?" he yelled.

"If I was y'all, I'd get out of there like my tail was on fire!"

"Let's go," Katía said.

Moving out the door, Fitz said, "Don't let go of him."

They ran through the smoke to find Ben and Zee standing over Earnie.

"How'd you find us?" Katía said, still hanging onto Everett's shirt.

"We figured they'd come back to check on the cows. Didn't expect to find you here, too," Zee said.

"You burnt down Daddy's barn," Everett groaned.

"Shut up, Everett," Earl said.

"What about the girls? Did anyone find them?" Katía asked.

"Yep. They came walking into the camp while we were looking for you," Ben replied.

"Thank God," Katía replied as she sank to a knee.

"We have to get away from the barn before the fuel blows," Fitz urged. They dragged the three boys past the front of the house.

"On the ground, all of you!" Fitz ordered. He rushed to Katía and helped her to sit down. "You're looking faint."

"I'm feeling it, too."

Fitz got onto his knees and leaned her back against his body. "We need an ambulance. Does one of you have a phone?"

"They're already on the way," Ben said. "Zee called when we first saw the smoke. I guess we ought to get your car out of the way."

Fitz wrapped an arm around Katía to steady her while he dug the key out of his pocket. He handed it to Zee, then rubbed Katía's arms. "Hang in there." He eased her onto her back.

Sirens overcame the increasing roar of the fire. Two minutes later lights strobed the smoke as two fire trucks, two ambulances, and two deputy cars pulled in one after the other.

A flurry of orders and movement created organized chaos. Two EMTs loaded Katía onto a stretcher and whisked her toward the ambulance to clear the area for the fire fighters. The deputies handcuffed the Inmansons and secured them in the cars.

Fitz hurried after Katía with Ben and Zee in tow. When they reached the ambulance, Katía chuckled, "Looks like I finally got my ducks in a row."

The three men laughed. With the gurney parked just behind the ambulance, one EMT assessed Katía while the other listened to Fitz's explanation of what she had been through. When they were ready to load her into the ambulance, she reached her hand out to Fitz.

He took it and said, "Don't you dare die on me."

"Don't worry, you're going to have to keep putting up with me."

An EMT from the second ambulance took Fitz by the arm. "Come with me, sir."

Fitz scowled at Ben, who shrugged his shoulders. "You haven't exactly had it easy the last twenty-four hours, either."

CHAPTER 43

Fitz hurried into the ER treatment bay and stopped at the side of Katía's bed, eyeing the IV line and cords running from the various monitoring devices. "Hey."

"Hey, yourself. I see they turned you loose. You OK?"

"I'm fine. How about you?" Ben and Zee had caught up and looked over his shoulder.

"Better now," she said reaching for Fitz's hand. He took it with both of his.

"I ain't never seen Fitz move as fast as he did on his way into the hospital," Zee chuckled. "Wait a minute," he eyed their hands. "What exactly happened in that cave?"

"Let's give them a minute," Ben suggested.

"You don't need to leave," Katía protested.

A nurse stuck her head in. "Ma'am, we have an unusual situation. There are two teenage girls and their families in the lobby begging to see you. They say you saved them. What would you like me to do?"

"I'd love to see them."

"It's irregular to have so many people back here. The rest of you will need to leave," the nurse added.

"I'm glad you're OK. We'll be back," Ben said as he and Zee walked out.

Fitz turned to go, but Katía didn't let go of his hand. "You're not going anywhere. Please send the girls on back."

The nurse shrugged her shoulders and went to get the girls. Sadie, her mother and father, Laurie, and her mom filed into the little room. Fitz moved to the wall at the head of the bed to give them room.

From opposite sides of the bed, Sadie and Laurie charged Katía, slowing down only to gauge how to weave their arms through the wires.

"How can I ever thank you for saving us? You risked your life, even though you didn't know us," Sadie gushed as tears rolled out of her eyes into Katía's hair.

Laurie choked out, "I've never been as grateful in my life."

Katía patted each girl on the back. "I just did what needed doing."

Sadie's dad cleared his throat and blinked his eyes. "We were afraid we'd never see our daughter again. She told us all that you did for her and how you comforted both of them. I'm eternally grateful to you, all of you, who had a hand in rescuing her. How can we ever repay you?" He nodded to Fitz, who nodded back.

Sadie's mom sobbed with a smile while Laurie's mom patted Katía on the knee. "I'm so grateful, too."

Sadie's mom took a deep breath to stem her sobs. "I can't tell you how much it means to me that you were kind to Sadie after all she's been through."

"Don't just stand there, Fitz. Get me a tissue," Katía said, tears flooding her eyes, too. She wiped her eyes and cheeks. "I'm sorry this happened to you two. It was terrible. Now you have to rebuild your souls so you can go out there and make your marks on the world. You are both wonderful people, and I'm grateful for the care you showed me."

"Can I have your number so we can stay in touch?" Sadie asked.

"Me, too," Laurie echoed.

Katía raised her eyebrows and looked at Fitz. "I don't have a phone anymore. I wonder what they did with it."

"They got mine, too," Fitz replied.

"I wonder if I can keep the same number. I sure hope so because a lot of people have it. Don't just stand there, Fitz. Find some paper and a pen."

Fitz looked around the room and inside the drawer of a little table. Before he got the drawer closed, he noticed Katía writing. She apparently noticed his confusion and said, "Laurie's mom."

After writing her number, she said, "OK, spill the beans. I'd like your numbers, too, … at least the ones you used to have." She wrote down the girls' numbers as well as those of their parents, just in case.

With final hugs the girls said good bye. As Sadie left the room, she turned and said, "I will get to see you again … at the trial." A mixture of pain and joy mingled in her expression.

"I'll definitely be there, and we'll have to get together for a meal or something," Katía replied. "Ooh! Y'all can stay at my house if you like!"

"We'd hate to impose, but that would be nice," Sadie's mom replied.

They left, and Fitz pulled up the chair and sat down facing Katía. "I don't know about you, but I'm beat."

"Yeah, me, too. I can't wait for a long sleep in my bed. It will feel so much better than being hogtied in that cave." She shuddered.

"It's going to take a while to get over that. I hope you don't have nightmares."

"Thanks for putting ideas in my head," she chided. "I can say one thing, I don't believe I've ever felt closer to God than when I was in that cave. I was more ready to move on to heaven than I could have imagined. Then I found that arrowhead and thought I was saved. Turns out, I was."

Fitz looked deeply into her eyes. Something shifted in the center of his chest, like chains breaking. The memory of the dream with Sharon in the coffin telling him it was OK flashed through as warmth spread through his body. Feeling lost in Katía's dark eyes, Fitz hardly realized he had leaned in close. Then his lips touched hers, and electricity tingled all the way to his fingertips.

"Well, bless my soul! Ain't that beautiful!"

Fitz jumped back as Zee and Ben walked into the little room.

"Maybe we should give them another minute," Ben said.

"No, you don't need to leave," Katía said, reaching for Fitz's hand. "It looks like this is what happened in that cave."

"Excuse me. Nurse coming through."

Ben and Zee stepped back to let the short, fortyish nurse get to Katía.

"I'm Rita. Are you folks family?" the nurse asked.

All three men shook their heads.

"I'll have to ask you to leave while I talk with Ms. Bancroft."

"It's OK. They can stay," Katía said.

"Well, OK, then. Everything in your blood work came back good and your lungs are clear. Those bruises will be painful for a while. Acetaminophen should help with that. As soon as this IV finishes, we'll get you out of here."

"Thank you. That sounds great."

"Do you have a ride home?"

"Ben Blessing's taxi service is at her disposal," Ben said with a smile.

"Great. I'll write up the paperwork." She marched out of the room with an efficient gait.

With the IV finished and discharge paperwork in hand, Katía transferred from the bed to a wheelchair. Ben took off to get the car, which he had parked in the lower level of the parking deck since Snickers and King were in there.

"I feel like I've been in a tornado and landed in Oz," Katía said, getting into the back seat of Ben's Outback. "Does anyone know where my car is?"

CHAPTER 44

Ben dropped Fitz off at the lower level of the hospital parking garage so he could get his car and Buffett. Fitz got into the car and announced to the cat, "We have to clean your litter."

Buffett rubbed him on the chin and purred. "Yeah, I missed you, too," Fitz said. After Buffett settled into his lap, Fitz stared at the wall in front of him. His world was discombobulated. He had missed his usual time at the library yesterday afternoon. He had not been sleeping regularly or eating on his usual schedule. But there was something else.

I kissed Katia. That thought plunked down into his soul like a puzzle piece clicking into place. Despite the smile it brought to his face, his thoughts whirled. *Why did I do that? What does that mean? Did she kiss me back? She definitely kissed me back. Is this the start of a relationship? What am I supposed to do?*

Buffett's meow broke the meandering march of his thoughts, and it dawned on him he was still sitting in the parking deck. *I'm supposed to be following them to Ben's.*

Fitz parked behind Katía's car in front of Ben's house. *Good, she hasn't left yet.* He hurried to harness Buffett and led him into the house. "Behave yourself," he told the cat after knocking on the door.

Walking into the house, he heard, "Oh, shoot! I never replied to Luna's text. She's going to kill me." It was Ben. Fitz found him in the den frantically typing on his phone.

"Glad you could make it," Katía said from her seat on the couch.

A surge of warring emotions hit Fitz all at once. It suddenly seemed loud and busy in the house. He was happy to see Katía but unsure how to behave. Panic welled up, and the room seemed far away and in a dark circle. *I have to get out of here.*

Katía's voice was soft and close. "It's OK, Fitz. Come and sit on the couch with me." She was holding his arm, then she took his hand. He did not realize he had backed all the way to the door. "Come on," she repeated. Her voice was soothing.

He let her lead him to the couch. She sat next to him, shoulders touching, and Fitz calmed down.

Zee appeared with two iced teas. "Congratulations on survivin' this ordeal. We're glad to have y'all back, smoochin' and everythin'."

Katía patted Fitz on the knee. "Relax. I think they figured it out."

Fitz took a sip of his tea and eyed Katía's hand. It was still on his knee. *What did they figure out?* He didn't want her to move her hand.

"I've been a hopin' you two'd get together. I'm just sorry it took nearly dyin' for that to happen."

Are we together? Fitz wondered. *I don't know how to be together.* He took another sip of his tea. His hand shook as he moved it to Katía's knee. He glanced at her, and she smiled, then took his hand in hers.

"You're shaking," she said.

Fitz nodded, not trusting his voice to respond. Setting her tea down, she rubbed his arm, and somehow it stopped trembling. He squeezed her hand, and she squeezed back.

"You're mighty quiet, Fitz. Drink your tea. You probably need fluids, too," Ben said.

Fitz took a big swallow. "I think you're right. My mouth is dry."

"Could just be nerves from sittin' next to this gorgeous woman," Zee added.

Katía spoke up. "Y'all, give Fitz a break. We sort of fell into this, and it's all brand new. It'll take some time to figure it out." She yawned. "Sorry. I can't wait to hit the shower and crawl into bed. It's been a long ordeal."

"You're all welcome to stay here tonight. It might be spooky staying by yourself. We can order pizza and a salad for supper."

"The thought of having to cook feels oppressive, and I am hungry," Katía said. "Pizza would be good."

There was a quick knock, then the front door popped open. Luna rushed in in a frenzy. "What happened? Are you OK? How did you get caught? How did you escape? What happened to the girls?" While the questions flew, she scurried around the room hugging everyone and finally landing on the couch. "You have to tell me everything."

She went wide-eyed when she noticed Katía and Fitz holding hands. "And I mean, you have to tell me EVERYTHING!"

Powering through three yawns, Katía recounted the story all the way to the present, including Sadie's and Laurie's visit to the hospital and the three Inmansons' arrests.

"I'm still waiting for the good part," Luna grinned, pointing at their hands.

"It seems this ordeal has brought us together," Katía said. "Fitz is my true knight in shining armor, even though I had gotten free before he got there." She elbowed Fitz. "There was something about that cave that drew me close to God and opened my eyes to my feelings for Fitz. It was terrible but quite mystical at the same time."

"I'm ordering pizza, do you want to stay, Luna?"

"That sounds great. Let me text Carlos and see if I can convince him to come."

While Luna was typing on her phone, Fitz felt Katía's head land on his shoulder. Her eyes were closed and her breathing was steady. His heart warmed that she would trust him enough to fall asleep next to him. He sat perfectly still so as not to wake her.

Ben took recommendations for what to put on the pizza. "I guess we'll just skip Katía. She needs the rest." He placed the order, and the park pals milled around chatting.

A gentle touch on Fitz's shoulder confused him. Opening his eyes, he discovered his head was laying over on Katía's. A dream evaporated, and Luna was telling him the pizza was here. "Wake up sleepy heads. It's time to eat," she said.

Katía sat up straight. "Wow. Sorry about that. I didn't mean to fall asleep."

"Don't worry about it," Ben replied. "You're going to need a lot of sleep to get over this."

Ben and Zee set up the food and other necessities on the counter. "You timed that perfectly," Ben teased when Carlos walked in right when everything was ready.

"Does anyone mind if I say a blessing?" Katía asked. With no objections, she proceeded. "Dear God, thank you for life and love and these friends. Thank you for getting us all through this ordeal safely and for providing this food. Amen."

"Let our two stars go first," Ben said, and Zee replied with, "Amen."

While Fitz picked out two slices of pizza and dished up some salad, the dream he was having when Luna awakened him returned to his memory. Sharon was in a field of daisies, picking them and putting them in her hair. She seemed so happy. She noticed Fitz standing on the edge of the field with Katía beside him. Fitz was afraid she would be mad, but she waved and said, "I hope you find as much joy as I have." That's when Luna woke him.

"Come on, Fitz. You're keepin' me from pizza," Zee said.

Fitz discovered he had stopped while holding the tongs in the salad. "Sorry." He took his plate and bowl and joined Katía at the table.

"A penny for your thoughts," she said. "What were you stuck on back there?"

"I was remembering a dream I had on the couch."

Katía grinned. "Is it something you can tell in public?"

"It wasn't that kind of dream."

"Bummer. If you want to share it, I'd love to hear."

Fitz took a bite of pizza to give himself time to think. *If we're going to be together, I need to share my thoughts.* Swallowing, he said, "OK. Do you remember me talking about Sharon?"

"Of course. She was the love of your life," Katía replied.

"Well… I was dreaming about her and you. She was in a field of daisies and very happy. She waved and wished us joy."

"Wow. That's profound, Fitz. Are you OK?"

He kissed her on the cheek. "Very."

"Cheers!" Ben said, holding up a glass of iced tea. The others held up their glasses with a round of cheers. "We've developed a tradition of getting together for a meal after surviving sticking our noses into dangerous cases. How about here on Saturday evening? I'll do the grilling."

"Where there's grillin', I'm always willin'," Zee said, holding up his glass again.

The others laughed and agreed with Zee.

CHAPTER 45

Katía announced she wanted to sleep in her own bed rather than stay at Ben's. Fitz fretted. He tried to convince her to stay. "What if they have accomplices that will want to silence you?"

She replied, "These guys aren't that sophisticated. They don't have accomplices."

Fitz still worried. He walked her to her car. The heat was still oppressive at 8:15. The sun painted the sky a weak pink having no clouds to use as a canvas.

When they reached her car, she took his hand. "I'm glad God opened my eyes to my feelings for you."

"Me, too." She did not make a move for the car door. *She's waiting. Is she waiting on me to kiss her? There's not but one way to find out.* With nerves tense, Fitz pulled her close, looked deeply into her eyes, then kissed her goodnight.

It was a delicious kiss, at least till the front door opened. Fitz pulled back and looked to see Luna and Carlos leaving.

"Don't let us stop you! See you in the morning at the park," Luna called and waved.

"Have a good evening," Katía replied.

Fitz nodded his head once, his arms still around Katía. When he realized he was still holding her, he let go and turned toward the others. "See you in the morning," he said.

"I need to get going," Katía said. "I'm worn out. I'll see you in the morning, too."

Fitz opened the car door. Once Katía was settled in the seat, he said. "It's going to be a long time till morning."

Fitz awoke disoriented. It was dark, and he was lying down rather than sitting back in his car. Buffett purred next to him. When his watch told him it was 6:42, he threw back the covers, covering Buffett. "Sorry, Bud." He hurried out of bed, donned his clothes in a rush, and headed for the front door.

"Good morning," Ben called from the kitchen, already holding a mug of coffee. Zee was at the counter eating a sweet roll.

"You gotta try one of these," Zee said.

"We're going to be late getting to the park," Fitz said.

"Relax, Fitz. You needed the rest. Have some breakfast while I text everyone that we're a bit behind schedule." Ben pulled out his phone to enter the text.

Fitz's feet were frozen where he stood. His heart pushed toward the door while his head and stomach pulled toward the sweet roll and coffee.

"Come on and have a seat," Ben said.

"Katía doesn't have a phone," Fitz replied.

"Oh, yeah," Ben said. "Here, at least take a sweet roll and some coffee to go." He was already pulling a travel mug from the cabinet. Zee hopped up and placed a sweet roll on a paper plate.

"Thanks," Fitz said. On the way to the door, he heard, "Meow."

"I think someone's head's in the clouds," Ben said.

"I almost forgot Buffett," Fitz puzzled. He harnessed him up and hurried to the car.

The sun was rising when he got to the park, painting the few clouds a marvelous coral. He let Buffett out and proceeded to wait. After a few minutes he said, "Let's sit at one of the picnic tables.

He watched as the sky changed hues, took a sip of coffee, then realized he missed his phone. "I've got to get a new phone today," he explained to Buffett.

"Meow."

Katía had not shown, prompting Fitz to get antsy. "Where could she be? I hope nothing's happened."

"Meow." Buffett rubbed Fitz's chin, then sat on the table to watch for chipmunks.

Finally lights appeared up the road. Fitz stood up. "It's just Ben and Zee," he explained to Buffett.

"It's seven-thirty. Where could she be?" Fitz asked as Zee placed treats on the ground for Buffett.

"I imagine she's still sleepin'. I'm sure the last couple of days took a lot out of 'er," Zee said.

"I agree with Zee. I think I'd sleep for two days if I'd been through being hogtied in a cave that long. She probably aches all over," Ben added.

"Let's go check on her," Fitz said.

"Ah, the sounds of newborn love. Ain't it sweet," Zee teased.

"One of you clowns find me her address," Fitz barked.

"You're testy this morning. I'll see if I can find an address for her, but I think you need to give her till lunch before you go storming over there," Ben replied.

"Here comes Luna," Zee noted. "At least give her till the end of our walk."

"Fine. I'll wait," Fitz grumped.

Luna got out of her 4Runner. "You all look so serious."

"Fitz is worried about Katía not bein' here yet," Zee replied.

"Poor thing. I'm sure she's exhausted. I'd be more worried if she were here. I'm making chocolate pecan pies for tomorrow."

"Yummy to my tummy!" Zee said.

Snickers tugged on the leash. "I know. We're coming, girl," Ben said. "She's ready to hunt some squirrels."

The group headed down the trail, Fitz lagging behind as they walked. *I hope she's OK. She said she would be here. Well, she said she would see me this morning. She didn't actually say she would be here. I'm sure she'd want to photograph this sunrise.*

A hand on his arm dragged him from his thoughts. "Come on. We'll go check on her as soon as we get back to the cars," Luna coaxed.

Fitz had not realized he had stopped. "OK." He kept pace with the group, wishing they would hurry up.

Back at the cars, Ben succeeded in finding an address for Katía. "I've got the address. Why don't all of you just ride with me?"

Ben instructed the dogs to get into the back, then the people loaded up. Buffett settled into Zee's lap.

"Traitor," Fitz said.

"He knows who's his buddy," Zee replied.

"He's just hoping for more treats," Ben added.

"Meow."

Ben parked in Katía's driveway. Fitz hurried to the door of the single-story brick house and knocked. When there wasn't a quick answer, he pounded harder.

"Patience is a virtue," Ben teased.

Fitz's nerves eased when he heard footsteps. Katía opened the door wearing a pink robe and pink slippers, hair definitely the bedhead look.

"What a wake-up committee," Katía said. "What's wrong?"

"You didn't show up at the park this morning, and Fitz got worried," Ben explained. "We tried to tell him you were sleeping in."

"I'm sorry, Katía. We had to make sure you were OK," Luna said. "We'll let you get back to bed."

"What time is it?" Katía asked.

"About eight-thirty-four," Fitz said.

"Wow. I haven't slept that late in a long time. Y'all want to come in and have some coffee?"

"We don't want to barge in on you. Since we know you're OK, we'll head on back to the park," Ben said, elbowing Fitz playfully.

"I'll be back at ten. We have to get new phones," Fitz stated.

Katía saluted. "Yes, sir." As he turned to walk back to the car, she added, "Thanks for checking on me. It's nice to know you care."

CHAPTER 46

It was 5:30 on Saturday afternoon when Ben lit the fire in both of his Weber grills. He had splurged on steaks for this celebration dinner. The potatoes were washed, poked, and ready to go into the oven. He sat down to take a break, going over in his mind each step that needed to be done in order to be ready for his guests. *I believe I'm set.*

The park pals were scheduled to arrive at 6:00, and at 5:50 the doorbell rang. Snickers gave her obligatory bark, and Ben answered the door.

"Come on in!" he said to Fitz, Katía, and Buffett. Fitz carried a bag with salad fixings for the meal.

"Hey, Ben, it's great to see you and great to be alive!" Katía said, giving him a hug. "Sorry we're a bit early. Fitz was excited to see everybody."

"I'm not sure 'everybody' is who Fitz was excited about," Ben grinned.

By 6:10, the whole group had assembled, including Laurie and her mom, Jenny, a forty-three-year-old blond who was obviously the mold for Laurie. Sadie and her family were back in Texas.

The group milled around, drinks in hand, while Ben tended to grilling the steaks. Luna had taken charge of the kitchen, preparing the salads and monitoring the timer for the potatoes.

Laurie gravitated to Katía. "Are you OK?" she asked.

"I'm getting there. Still a bit tired and sore. How about you? How are you handling all of this?" Katía responded.

The rest of the group gathered around Laurie.

"I'm still addled. I can't believe they just grabbed me in the middle of the day like that. Right out in the open. I probably won't be able to go to school Monday. I don't think I'll ever be able to ride the bus again."

Jenny put her hand on Laurie's shoulder. "I think going to school would be the best thing you can do. Get back to your routine, see your friends. It'll help."

"I think she's right," Carlos added.

"Gee, thanks," Laurie chuckled. "It was worth a try."

"Did you ever figure out why they kidnapped you and Sadie?" Luna asked.

Laurie crossed her arms. "They thought they could charm us into wanting to marry them. They kept saying they'd train us to be farm wives."

"That's creepy," Ben said, having a few minutes before the steaks needed flipping. "I'm just grateful they didn't do anything … you know, worse than holding you prisoner."

"We're all grateful and amazed about that," Jenny said, giving Laurie a quick hug.

"Yeah, they didn't seem that evil, well, except for Earl. He was mean as a snake. Everett was actually kind of nice. I'm sure he could have gotten a girlfriend the normal way."

Katía chuckled. "Everett, poor thing. He sure was worried about what his mama would have thought."

"Yeah, it was smart how you kept using that to manipulate him," Laurie said.

Fitz's new phone rang. It was the sheriff's office. He scrunched his eyes and answered.

"Hey, Fitz! Sheriff Tucker here."

"Hey, Sheriff. What's up?"

"We got a complaint about you. It appears some folks living on the lake identified you on their property from their security cameras."

Fitz looked to Zee and mouthed, "Uh, oh."

"They wanted to press charges till I explained that you were there trying to locate an abducted girl. Please tell me that's what you were doing."

"That's exactly right," Fitz replied.

"Anyway," Sheriff Tucker continued, "There wasn't any damage, so they agreed not to pursue charges. They were puzzled about the guy in the ski mask. Any idea who that was?"

"He would prefer to remain anonymous," Fitz chuckled. He explained the call to the group, then Jenny picked up the conversation where they had left off.

"I can't believe they built a room with no doors. That's pure evil," Jenny said.

"You gotta admit, it was a clever design, though," Zee added.

Everyone looked at Zee like he was looney, then they laughed. "You're right, Zee," Luna said.

"The worst part was when they put you in that cave. I can't believe they really left you there to die," Laurie said. "That's when I knew they really were evil." She wrapped her arms around Katía.

Fitz looked away and wiped his eyes.

"They stuck ole Fitz in there, too. I sure am glad Katía got y'all out of there with that arrowhead," Zee added. "Turns out, it must've been a magic cave to get the two of you together."

Fitz scrunched his eyebrows, wishing Zee would hush.

"Wait, you two are a couple?" Laurie put her hand over her mouth. She reached and pulled Fitz in, keeping the other arm around Katía. "That's wonderful! I can't wait to tell Sadie!" She whipped her phone from her back pocket and initiated the text.

Katía sidled up to Fitz and put an arm around his waist. "When they stuck me in that cave, they said it was a 'dying cave.' Turns out, it was really a living cave."

A NOTE FROM THE AUTHOR

I really appreciate you for investing your time in reading this book and trust it was enjoyable. It would mean a lot to me if you would take a moment to go to the site from which you purchased the novel and leave a review or at least a rating.

If you enjoyed my writing and would like to get notified of new releases, please sign up for my newsletter on the website: www.dwainwrites.com. You get a free eBook that tells the story of Fitz's life during the time he met Sharon with a newsletter sign-up. On the website, you can also learn more about me and my other books.

Happy reading and happy living!
Dwain

ACKNOWLEDGEMENTS

Numerous people were helpful in bringing this book from an idea to fruition. B. J. Myers-Bradley, Clara Bella Rose, and Yvette Summerour were gracious with their time, read through the manuscript, and provided feedback that made this a better story. I truly appreciate their time and insights.

I am deeply grateful to Merilyn Guerry for applying her skills to editing the manuscript. I never cease to be amazed at her grammatical prowess and attention to detail!

I am grateful for the artistic skills of Becky Franks for the author photo. The cover creation was a collaboration between Lap Cat Publishing and Getcovers.

BOOKS BY DWAIN CASSADY

THE PARK PALS SERIES:
THE HIDDEN SCALPEL
THE MISSING PILL
THE DYING CAVE
TWO STOLEN MEN

THE DARK WINGS TRILOGY:
DARK WINGS RISING
DARK WINGS DARING
DARK WINGS SOARING

THE WILLOW NOVELS:
FEATHERS IN WATER
FEATHERS IN FLIGHT

ADVENT DEVOTIONALS:
INSIGHTS FROM MATTHEW
PRESENCE IN THE MANGER
THE COMING LIGHT
THE SOIL OF SALVATION